NANCY | NIANCI

A Story of Wars

"I have just finished *Nancy/Nianci,* but it won't leave my head for a long time. An un-put-down-able book, one that speaks to every person's heart."

— SUSAN MORRIS,
The Notting Hill Book Club

"A saga for the ages. It illuminates a tragic period in history that should be better understood."

— JULIE J. KIDD,
President, Endeavor Foundation

"Loved it. A very powerful book. The story is a remarkable one; in fact, I think you have just scratched the surface."

— RICHARD CHOW,
author, formerly head of EnergyWorks Asia

"I was up way too late with *Nancy/Nianci* — so compelling, and beautifully written."

— ERICA JOHNSON, M.D.

"I found the story fascinating from start to finish."

— JAMES M. STONE,
author of Five Easy Theses

"A gripping, vivid, courageous, heart-rending, historic, touching — I could go on — story."

— ANDREW LEVY

To the memory of Zhou Nianci

CHAPTERS

Through the great Gate

Along the towered Wall

By the banks where ducks preened in winter sun

We rode.

You lifted the reins.

Swiftly you drew away.

Your cry came back in the wind.

That Gate, that Wall are levelled.

Wind stirs the dust.

Wind whispers the echo

Of you to me

Of me to you.

—WILMA CANNON FAIRBANK

PREFACE

What happens if time's up and your story is still locked inside you? You haven't told your story, not as a whole, maybe not even in pieces. Maybe you've written down parts of it, but most of it is untold. Left untold, time will wash it away.

When she was still youthful, without any warning my mother *Zhou Nianci* was suddenly felled by a massive stroke. It rendered her mute and severely incapacitated. She kept her mind and her spirit, but gone was something of rare value: the chance for her to delve into her strikingly unusual story, to tell us the details she'd spent a lifetime glossing over. And for us to understand exactly why she'd left China.

She was a writer, but she'd lost her voice. For most of her adult life, her voice was muffled by wartime politics, and then by decades of Cold War. Then, just as the Cold War ended, and my mother could begin to speak, vigorously seeking a publisher for her writings—the stroke took away her newly regained voice.

Committed to restoring her voice, now that her story can be told—thanks to changed circumstances, the passage of time, and earlier disclosures by family—I've pieced together her story. It's based on what she'd previously shared, what she'd written down, and what I learned through research. She'd told us little about the grim particulars of the experience of her family—my family—in China: China in devastating wartime, from the 1930s through World War II and beyond. In defiance of the wars that had dominated her life, my mother named me Peace, or *An,* in Chinese. My

Chinese surname is *Bian,* for Bennett, my father's surname. My parents chose to raise their children as American, not Chinese, for reasons of politics and racial discrimination. So *Bian An* became Ann Bennett.

This book is written in the voice of *Nianci Zhou (Zhou Nianci),* or Nancy Bennett, as she was later known to Americans. Not only is the voice adopted, but it speaks as though in the moment. The reader sees intense personal challenges amid historically significant events—events that still shape our world today. Of course, their future importance was not perceived in their moment: you live your life making choices based only on what's known at the time. Sometimes, even with the wisdom of hindsight, you can't look back, because current circumstances are so urgent. Or so painful.

Zhou Nianci lived a full life, yet also a life of upheaval and loss, of war and immigration, racial discrimination and crushing disappointment. She remained determined, upbeat, unbroken. She wrote memoirs, poetry, and fiction. This book is an effort to give her the voice she lost.

Some of Nianci's writings are excerpted in this book, as ***indented and bold italics in quotes.*** The book is a novel that describes Nianci's experience. It's a work of historical fiction that reconstructs personal events as understood by the author. Certain names have been changed, and characters and actions are presented subject to the author's interpretation and memory. *Nancy|Nianci* is dedicated to Zhou Nianci, and to her enduring legacy.

—Ann Bennett Spence
(*Bian An*)
2021

CHAPTER 1

War Is a Living Thing and It Brings Death

We're in Peking, 1936. Up north, the Imperial Japanese Army is five years into its invasion of China, fighting its way south from Manchuria toward Peking. In Europe, Nazi Germany has begun marching eastward, taking the Rhineland. The Olympics are unfolding at Munich, where Hitler mesmerizes audiences on a world stage. Some Japanese military and undercover men are already here in Peking, mingling with Chinese plainclothesmen and the sinister political police wearing darkest blue. People are fearful, but it's dangerous to speak of it openly. The Chinese Nationalist Army is camped near our college campus just outside the city, mustering a showy effort to defend Peking against Japan's so-called Rising Sun. It's unclear who's friend and who's enemy, because there are many sides to this war in China, and the streets of Peking are murky with fear.

I'm Nianci, and I write what I see going on around me.

Yesterday they released C.T. from the prison downtown and he made his way back to campus. He says he was beaten, tortured even, but that he told them nothing. That's what he says. I don't know what to believe any more—whether or not he was actually tortured and kept his mouth shut about what we're up to. Whether he's with us or with the Japanese now. Maybe he's always been one of the spies we've been told to watch out for, and the soldiers roughed him up just to make him look like he's our friend. But he *is* my friend, even my boyfriend for awhile until I decided on George instead. All those hours C.T. and I used to spend together, talking about what's happening all around us, getting closer and closer so that it was starting to get dense and physical, and now I have to look back and wonder. Maybe he was just trying to get me to talk about what I'm doing with my writings and with the plans for speaking out.

Or maybe it's all just personal, not political at all. Maybe C.T. just wants me to think he's a hero for not breaking down under whatever the soldiers did. But he does seem to stand less tall now. He's jumpy when he didn't used to be. I bet he's not going to talk back next time a Japanese soldier shoves him or demands to see his I.D. or even asks for his money. I'm not going back to C.T., not leaving George, at least not yet.

All the world is in front of me, so much to do, so much to find out about, to write about, so many friends, so many boyfriends. I'm 20. I came to college here at Yenching University as a "local", meaning my family lives in Peking. Even though my family is well-known, I'm one of the first girls in the family to go to college. In China it's unusual for girls to go to college, but my father has seen Europe and America and I'm a good student. Plus, I'm the oldest child and I was starting to talk back about some Chinese traditions. Such as arranged marriages. My mother would sit stony-faced when these disagreements came up, but my father thought the solution was to send me off to college, where I can live in a girls' dormitory away from home. He's stalling for time, but it won't work. Because college just opens up new worlds for me.

To me, Peking is vast and stretching to all horizons, in one direction the streets jammed with people in plain cottons, loudly haggling in street markets zig-zagged by rickshaws bearing the rich on their way to comfortable homes or male-only clubs or the Grand Hotel de Pékin. In another direction there's the looming city wall, ancient before the hills stretching beyond. In yet another direction the Forbidden City, with spiky grass growing between its roof tiles, buildings shabby now from neglect and disrespect, now that the Empire has fallen and China has soldiered up with guns and swords and knives and even farm implements, anything out of nothing, anything to fight back as the Japanese invasion grinds on and on.

College started out with so much promise. I'm lucky to come from a family that believes education is more important than money, even for a girl. Yes, Yenching University supposedly has a lot of rich kids, and yes it was started by a bunch of American missionaries, and yes the beautiful buildings were built partly by American money. But most of the faculty are Chinese, the things we study and dream of are Chinese, we think and speak Chinese, we *are* Chinese and we are bound to be leaders in China once we finish our education. Or at least the boys are; the girls are bound to marry these leaders. The men at Yenching outnumber the women by around three to one, so I'm used to being surrounded by these young men of promise. But I know I have promise too, and I'm starting to see that others might be expecting more of me than "just a girl." People listen to me because I'm smart and I have stories to tell, even though I'm only 20.

I have my family story, my famous grandfather Liang Qichao—but more of that later. I also have the story, I mean I *write* the story, of China being attacked by the Japanese, at first grabbing Manchuria in the north five years ago when I was practically just a kid. Now there are hundreds of thousands of Japanese soldiers in China, not just up north; they're showing up in Peking. Soldiers are in the streets, sometimes hitting Chinese with their gun butts, shouting in their strange language, pushy and vulgar. We can be vulgar too; we call them the "island dwarfs" but we're careful to say that beyond their hearing because they can haul you off to prison when they're provoked. Or kill you.

C.T. didn't call them names when they stopped him in the street. He just refused to hand over his money. They hauled him off. Some of these Japanese soldiers are just boys too, but nasty boys. They're hungry, I mean hungry for food. They roam all over the countryside and beat up peasants and steal their food and animals, wringing the head off a chicken and flaming the bird whole on an outdoor fire right in front of starving children. Sometimes they're hungry for things besides food, like sex. Some of them rape when they think they can get away with it. They act like savages. And more and more of them are coming into Peking. The Japanese forces are *here* and they're in charge, I don't care what our local government says. Our government might as well admit they're just puppets and Japan's pulling the strings. When Japanese soldiers stop us in the streets or push us or rob us or worse, our local police just look the other way.

So, this is 1936, and I write articles about how our country is being invaded and ground down by these savage imperialists who are even worse than any western imperialists in our past. And about how our government isn't doing enough to fight back. *China must be saved!* I say that all the time. My writings are published in pamphlets and youth newspapers that allow students to write articles. In the west (but mainly in their churches) they're very interested in how we "noble Chinese" are faring under the heel of the Japanese tyrant, and they read some of my opinions and stories. But let's face it, most westerners are far more worried about the Nazi jackboot than about Japan. Germany's on the march, and the Brits and Americans are wide awake to that nightmare. But Japan's march is just an afterthought to them. China is so vast, they say—what are even a half-million Japanese soldiers going to do to China? They'll just get bogged down in the rice paddies, they say.

But those westerners aren't *here,* and they have no idea. They don't know fear in these teeming, begging streets, the sometimes violent police, the sinister warlords, and always those Japanese soldiers. *Death by battle, death by torture, death by beatings, death by robbery, death by execution, death by rape, death by disease, death by starvation, death by deliberate flooding, death by bombing.* My beloved uncle Sizhong, who graduated from West Point, was in China's 19th Route Army which was defending Shanghai. He was killed in 1932 by the Japanese, and I was shocked because he'd had all that military training. But I was just a kid then, and the Japanese invasion had just begun. Later I decided that of all the westerners, it's especially the Americans who are so innocent. West Point training doesn't work in China. Americans are smart, and they can be generous, but they are naive. They ignore what the Japanese army is doing to China. They even sell war stuff to the Japanese. They have no idea.

Last December, I was part of something that's already being described as an historic event: the December 9th Movement. Along with hundreds of my classmates I marched from my college to Peking, in defiance of the government authorities and the Japanese. It was perishing cold even in our winter padded clothing. Cold to the bone. We held up white banners or gripped our mittened hands in front of ourselves to keep them warm and ready to push back if Japanese soldiers or the government police tried to shove us or arrest us or beat us. The wife of an American journalist later wrote that "thousands and thousands of blue-clad youngsters marched and sang their way to the Forbidden City in defiance of their own police and conservative parents. Chinese shopkeepers, housewives, artisans, monks, teachers and silk-gowned merchants applauded from the streets, or ran out to get leaflets [from the students]. Even rickshaw coolies shouted the forbidden slogans: *'Down with the bogus independence movement! Down with Japanese imperialism! Save China!'*"

Some of my friends were arrested or beaten right there on the spot—mostly boys, hardly any girls. But one of the girls is a close cousin of mine, Sukie, and she *was* beaten, with a sword and by a policeman. The sword was in a scabbard, but still the beating was vicious. Sukie's in her junior year at Yenching, a year older than me, and as children she and I had always played together. I'll never forget her bravery that day—she never cried, just stuck out her chin and glared. Beaten down to her knees, Sukie was arrested and jailed for two days. Now that the Japanese authorities have her name, they'll be watching her closely, finding any excuse to arrest her again. So she's telling her friends and me that she wants to escape from Peking, maybe go to the caves in Yan'an where the Communists are headquartered—or even to America.

I worry too. I'd marched at the front of the procession that day—see, here's a photo—helping lead the demonstration. Yenching students protesting the Japanese invasion! Protesting the Nationalists for not fighting the Japanese! We are *all* Chinese, not just the Nationalists, but the Communists too. After the demonstration, we students meet often, to organize and print posters and write pamphlets against the Japanese invasion. We soon join in with students in other universities in China, and so a broad student movement is started. We demand to be heard.

For many of us, this December 9th Movement was our first experience with politics and danger. It was our first involvement in the tensions between the Nationalists who are supposedly running our government, and the Communists who were forced by the Nationalists to flee their headquarters in Shanghai, for the distant caves of Yan'an. An American, Edgar Snow, who teaches journalism at Yenching and who wants to visit Yan'an, has told us that these Communists are idealistic and determined to win against the Japanese. They fight, but in skirmishes and not flat-out, because the Communists (unlike the Nationalists) have hardly any weapons, and the Japanese are armed to the teeth. The Communist "peasant soldiers," many of them recruited only recently, have courage driven all the more by starvation. We students are impressed with the way this Red Army is standing up for China. Some of my friends, including C.T., say they want to join the Communist Party and even think about traveling to Yan'an to stand with the Communists and fight the Japanese. Some other students, and especially their parents, call the Red Army the "Red Bandits"—and like the President, Chiang Kai-shek, they seem just as much against the peasant army as against the Japanese Army. I think it's ridiculous to have Chinese fighting Chinese. We should all be fighting against the Japanese.

Life in Peking is tough right now, but life in the rural areas is far worse. In Peking we're made shabby by the invaders, we have street brutality and bullies and nasty Japanese soldiers, and sometimes people disappearing in the night, random dead bodies in the streets in early morning, routinely dragged and thrown onto donkey carts. And we have inflation so bad that your money has been stolen from you before you're even paid. But in Yan'an you're living in caves, far away from anyone you know, no news, harsh living by any standard. Yet we're told there's a discipline and spirit there, a fighting spirit that won't be quelled by any invader. That's why some are going to join with the Communists.

I won't go to Yan'an though. I'm a city girl. I want to be near newspapers and other ways to fight with words. The Communists use a lot of wall posters—pictures of muscled peasants with upheld fist—because most of the peasants can't read. Not much writing in the rural areas. I'm going to stay in the city to continue to write my political articles, and I'll fight this way instead.

My parents are angry, seething at me now, especially my mother. She thinks I've completely run off the rails, spending way too much time at student meetings. These meetings are sometimes just faculty and students gathering at a faculty member's home. We sip tea and we talk. Sometimes we drink something stronger. We do talk politics, of course. We talk about what we can do to save China from the invaders. We ask why the American government isn't helping China. American officials say nice things about China and help the Nationalists get American weapons, but they don't speak out against the Japanese colossus that's stomping all over us. What are the Americans waiting for? They cry for China, but it's only crocodile tears because we're too far away for them to care enough to *do* anything. They think Europe is closer than Asia. They're wrong, I know they're wrong.

But my parents think this is all too much for me, because I'm just a sophomore, and just a girl, and what do I know. I'm supposed to be reading at the library, studying for my exams, and at worst going to parties. They don't want me to curl my hair or wear makeup (like so many of my girlfriends) or wear western clothing. So, I don't wear makeup. When I go to parties, I wear a *qipao,* the Chinese-style slinky dress, but I don't mind because it clings to my body and the dress has a pretty high slit on each side to show off my legs, so I can deal with the false modesty of the high collar. When I walk, especially when I wear higher heels, I notice people noticing me, especially the young men. Even some slightly older men in their 30s. But I'm not so much pretty as just plain interesting, whether I'm at a political meeting or at a tea dance at the Grand Hotel where even the western men—maybe especially the western men—find girls like me fascinating, mesmerizing even. I can tell.

When my mother found out that I was in the student march last December, she rushed over to my uncle and aunt's home, near the university, where I often stay overnight. She demanded that I return home immediately to be straightened out. She was so angry she just spat out her words at my aunt and me. Some background here: my mother has always put my aunt at a distance, because she disapproves of her "western ways." But my aunt is Lin Huiyin, a famous poet, and she's magnetic. My uncle is Liang Sicheng, and he's an expert on Chinese architecture. He teaches at Tsinghua University which is practically next door to Yenching. In fact—and this is what angers my mother so much—Huiyin and I are actually close friends, because she's not that much older than I am. She and my uncle Sicheng were even married at our home, when I was 14. It was an arranged marriage, and it's one reason I don't want my parents picking a husband for me.

Huiyin! I want to be just like her, but I wouldn't want to be stuck the way she is. She's had a complicated life, and a lost love, and I know she's torn between traditional family strictures and her own fiercely independent nature. It's the freedom I want, not all the family rules. My mother sees my closeness to Huiyin, and like a match it lights her fury. My mother's all about rules, and she's afraid I'll become as independent as Huiyin, who wears scandal in a way that just adds to her stature.

When I was a child, if I misbehaved, my mother's anger and staring silence would terrify me. Her mouth can be a slit and her big eyes completely unblinking, a long and silent stare, aimed at me. But now I'm learning to defy her. I no longer shrink. I talk back. More and more, I go my own way, without telling anyone. Sometimes I might try to get my father's tacit agreement, but he's usually too busy to listen for long, and besides he can be full of rules too. He teaches law. He walks ramrod straight and when angry he can put people down with withering remarks.

My father's respected, looked up to; people come to our house to meet with him behind closed doors. From stray remarks, I know they're talking about the Japanese—the Japanese who attempt to hide their invasion behind the mask of collaboration. My father makes it clear that he'll never collaborate, never accept a position seized or invented by Japan to govern China. He's tough, and plenty shrewd. Maybe he sees in me some of his own scrappiness and independence. But unlike my mother, he isn't alarmed by this, and his eyes are almost never harsh. They flash knowingness and sometimes even humor. This gives me hope that if family rules become too tight, he'll be on my side.

My mother disapproves of the faculty and student gatherings at Sicheng and Huiyin's place. She's caught a glimpse of rebel in me, and she worries I'll fall into non-traditional relationships, such as with a particular older man she thinks has his eye on me. But actually, he's more interested in Huiyin, who's ravishing in her silky slim dress and has a smile that flashes with dimples that seem to drive the men wild. Naturally my mother had suspected the worst—that this man, actually a philosophy professor, was after *me*. And that I was becoming a radical, a student with a voice too loud, a marcher and a writer and possibly even a fallen woman. That's why she rushed over to drag me back home.

So little she knew. She never even saw the photo of me marching all puffed out in padded winter gown, *not* sexy, but with curled hair. I finally curled it, as a way of rebelling. So what if it's "too western"; it's not up to my mother to decide what's right for me. Or my famous family, who (along with my ancestors) are constantly being invoked by my mother. To her fury, I've asked my friends to call me Nancy.

Home is a trap, ready to ensnare me. My future there is hoary with tradition, but utterly clear: my mother may be Liang Qichao's daughter, and Liang an authority on the West, but still she's Old China. She wants a Chinese courtship for me, a Chinese marriage complete with a mother-in-law to keep an eye on me, and plenty of baby boys. The man I marry must be chosen, or at least approved, by my father—with my mother's agreement. He must be from "a good Peking family." I'm their only daughter, and now that I'm almost 21 they're worried that I'm well on my way to becoming a spinster, a *lao chu nü* that no one wants. Ha! What do they know.

My three younger brothers are useless in all this, because boys aren't stuck with being sent to another family like a dutiful servant. I refuse to be servant to some man and his mother. My father says don't exaggerate, my mother lapses into her cold stare. But off to the side, I do have an ally of sorts, and I call her *Po*. And here it gets complicated, because Po is my grandfather Liang's second wife and widow. My grandmother was Liang's first wife, and Po was initially her "handmaiden". Later Po became my grandfather's concubine. Po's only a few years older than my mother, and my mother has always disliked her. Everything my mother is not, Po is: warm, close, relaxed. Blessed with a lively sense of humor, she's watched me grow, listened to my stories of triumphs and setbacks, and most of all to my complaints about my strict mother. She's on my side, but she's careful to hide that when my parents and I differ.

So home is a trap. I escaped to college. Now events at college are sucking me in, pulling me away from my father, my mother, my whole family. Yenching was always a beacon, a place to be free of my parents, to discover new people and new issues. But now it's become a vortex.

I've already said I'm smart, which is a good thing because I'm not beautiful at all, and I'll never turn any heads that way. But when I get together with other students, when we talk about issues and I tell my stories and speak my mind, I can see them changing the way they look at me, the boys especially. They're interested. The boys are downright amazed at a girl who speaks so urgently of the same issues that they do. No one who's near me is ever bored, because I can catch fire. I catch it all the time. I know some young men here who want to get to know me better.

I also have many women friends not only because we're "pioneers" (according to the white-haired white-suited American who established this university and who thinks Chinese women deserve a college education), but also because we share stories and all kinds of decisions. Like what to do about the war, what to do if the young man you like is wishy-washy about the war. Which side are you on, the Nationalists or the

Communists or one of the other political parties? We talk about the students we know—especially the ones who might be spying for the Japanese. And what about our teachers, the faculty? Who can be trusted?

Is it crazy just to sit here while the Japanese army is getting ready to attack Peking full-on? How to escape before they do that? We mull over the same old limited choices: go west to the Communist base in Yan'an, or even farther west to Kunming in "Free China", or southeast to Nanjing the capital city, or eastward to the ocean to find passage on a ship from Tianjin to carry us away from the terrors of collaboration and occupation. Or should we just continue to stay put, either burying our faces in books or speaking out the way I've been doing?

Now the enemy has circled Peking and they're rattling their swords, barely to the north of us, each day recruiting more collaborators among the elite of Peking (and Yenching is full of elites). Japanese soldiers walk ever more freely in our streets, individually and in packs. My father tells me to be careful, not to become a target for the enemy, like my cousin Sukie. After he learned of my joining in the December 9th Movement, he almost didn't allow me to come back to Yenching for my junior year. So now I try to be more careful about the meetings and pamphlets, because I don't want my father to stop paying my college fees.

I'm determined to keep writing articles for student newspapers, but now I'm domesticated. I try to keep my writing nonpolitical while still colorful:

"Dong, dong, dong, dong! The big gong strikes 'four bells.' Before the hollow tones die out, the janitor has started the dormitory bell. Up and down the corridors

he goes, ringing mercilessly, dinning the metallic noise into sleeping brains. Doors start banging...Now the bathroom wakes in earnest. With strange hisses, and gurgles, hot-water taps begin working; they roar into bathtubs as they are turned on full force. Washbasins and all sorts of other useful articles connected with washing rattle in the midst of the din. A soap-dish crashes to the floor, followed by a loud yell and much laughter. An ambitious voice rises in song. A piercing shriek of the power-house whistle announces seven-thirty. Even the laziest of those with first-hour classes have to get up now. And when they do, everybody cannot help but know it. Flinging their doors shut with a violence that shakes the whole building, they rush up the stairs for breakfast."

When I send these kinds of things to American news publishers, they are always interested. Their readers are interested in "a young voice of China," one that speaks English. They cluck over China's plight ("a pity, a pity") but they don't ask their government to help us. So I write plenty of innocuous descriptions of life at my university, the kind of thing that appeals to readers of the very popular *Reader's Digest* in America, hoping that sympathetic American readers will see we're like them, and that we need help against the Japanese invaders.

Meanwhile, here at university I'm now going to events that are more social, like receptions and tea parties where the talk is of books and literature and plays, not about politics. Or not *just* about politics. After all you can't escape politics when the servant who picks up the teacups looks like he's starving, or maybe he leans closer because he's one of those spies we're always being warned about. Spies working for the Japanese.

It's always politics. But still I try to be social: besides tea parties, and receptions with rice wine or that German beer from Tsingtao, there are still courtyard dances at the Grand Hotel de Pékin, thinning out now, where among the potted palms we students seek the dance floor, trying to forget the war.

I still go to see Huiyin, who loves art and writes poetry. She'll always be my friend, no matter my mother's disapproval. I can tell her anything, and she leans forward, bright-eyed, full of encouragement. Sometimes she sits me down to read poetry together and she speaks of a complex life. When it's just the two of us talking by firelight, I sometimes see that her face is pale and detached from the smile, and there's bleakness, something lost behind her eyes. In one of the poems she's written for me, she says she was inspired by the sight of happy college students, which is what I think she sees in me. She sees the future in me, and in my friends, while in her there's a sense of something past, something taken away, whose memory never quite leaves her.

That memory is Xu Zhimo, the poet and her close friend, maybe too close they say, who died in a plane crash five years ago while on his way to Peking. Huiyin had waited at the airport to meet him, and it was there she learned he'd never arrive. In her sad moments with me, Huiyin speaks of him both obliquely and directly. Her marriage to my uncle had been arranged by their two fathers, and I see there are times when she feels bound too tight, shackled by family and tradition. Her voice is unhappy when she calls me "Little Cinnamon," the nickname my grandfather gave me, which refers to a rabbit companion to the Moon Goddess of Chinese legend, sitting under a cinnamon tree.

Yet like me, Huiyin brightens whenever there's a gathering, and now she gathers me up along with my student friends, to go shopping at the street markets. She shows us how to look for beautiful porcelains and small relics and other treasures thrown up by war and pillage and the rifling of temples and tombs. Church icons from St. Petersburg and Moscow, sold by desperate White Russians who fled to China. Candlesticks of bronze or of black iron, spirited away from Buddhist temples. Painted wooden masks, clay statuary, and fine silks lushly embroidered with fanciful bats and flowers. The black market and smugglers profit from war and disruption, she says, and why not find this treasure and bring it back to where it's appreciated, maybe someday even placed in a museum.

So we wander the markets surrounded by wafting incense and tang of street food, the dissonant insults of buyers and sellers in full-throttle bargaining amid the sounding of temple bells and the chatter of parrots trained to utter auspicious words in perfect Mandarin. The market streets are unpaved, and the occasional dusty camel plods by, hood-eyed and mournful—or sometimes an entire slow caravan of camels, hauling the coal that's used for heating and cooking. Bicycles weave through the clutter. Such color, such din, such crowding of human toil for money, however gained and however meager.

The war looms over our attempts to forget its reach, and it leers at our efforts to ignore it. I look up and I see a gaping ogre's mouth, ever-widening above our city, slowly making ready to devour us.

CHAPTER 2

War Menaces

And then I meet Joshua, that fall of 1936. He's an American, one of those well-meaning but naive and awkward Americans who speak Chinese just well enough to try to order food at a restaurant, but not to know what the food's about. They ask for "chow mein" and then sit amazed that the restaurant has never heard of it. But before we get to the restaurant part, I must tell how we even met in the first place. Like me, he's in his junior year at Yenching, but he's here only for this one year. I first see him in the library where he was checking out some books. I don't think he noticed me at all, but I sure noticed him because there are so few white students here, and besides he's so good-looking, like that actor in the movie "Of Human Bondage." Back in the dorm, my girlfriends and I all agree that he's definitely someone worth meeting, but how?

That problem is solved because it turns out that he later saw me ice-skating on the lake. (Just as background, I'm very athletic—swimming, running, ice skating). The lake is called No Name Lake, in the middle of our campus. Because I'm such a good skater, Joshua asked someone who I was. Not that he came up to me right then. It's later that we meet, at one of those gatherings at Huiyin's and Sicheng's home:

"Nancy, *Nancy*, I want you to meet this very nice young man who tells me that he's here from America and a classmate of yours!" says Huiyin, all dimples and charm. "His name is Joshua Bennett. Joshua, this is my niece and good friend Nancy Zhou, the best young writer in all of Yenching!" with typical lilting overstatement. Huiyin always calls me Nancy now.

Joshua—tall, thin, with impossibly wavy hair—squirms slightly but gamely tries out some Mandarin on me. His words are correct but his pronunciation a bit off when he says, "Pleased to meet you" and grins with such delight that I just want to keep the conversation going.

I switch back to English (he looks miffed but gets over it) and I say, "I think I saw you in the library the other day, and I wondered who you were."

"I saw you ice skating yesterday, and I wondered the same thing."

Huiyin laughs lightly, "So this was meant to be!" and hurries off to tend to other guests.

Joshua asks me the usual, where I'm from, what I'm studying, do I know so-and-so. I do the same. He says Nancy sounds like "a rather American name," and I say that my real name is Nianci—Nancy's just the English version of Nianci. I learn he started college at Harvard, which happens to have a connection to Yenching, so I think he can't be stupid. But then he says he left after freshman year to go to a university in California called UCLA—never heard of it, but I'm too tactful to say so. In any case, it was at UCLA that he decided to stop trying to study China from so far away, but just to *go* to China instead. To Yenching University.

"So here I am," he says, looking exhilarated as he glances all around the room, as though trying to gulp down everything he's seeing, his curiosity about everything almost wild on his face. Ready for adventure.

"You picked an interesting time to come to Peking," I say, "what with Japanese soldiers everywhere and a war going on. Not exactly a holiday."

"I'm not looking for holiday. I want to learn, and I'm not afraid of fascists. I wrote about them in my school newspaper." My ears prick up. "The Japanese army is no different from the German one, if you ask me," he says.

And so we plunge into talk about the Nazis in Germany and Japan's terrible but undeclared war raging in China, how I've been writing about it for student publications, how my parents are afraid I'll overstep and get myself arrested, how I don't care about that, how I care more about *China* and the way I see it Japan wants to destroy China to steal our coal, and their puppet government in Manchuria is doing exactly that. I speak passionately, and I can see Joshua drawing closer, more and more interested.

We leave the party, Huiyin looking a bit anxious by now about the intensity of my huddle with Joshua, no doubt worrying that my mother could make another raging visit to lambaste her for exposing her daughter to dangerous influences, to people with political talk and (even worse) *westerners* with political talk.

From that evening on, Josh (he's asked that I call him "Josh") seeks me out nearly every day, whether at my dorm, in the library, in classes, or on the pathways between. Sometimes we meet for a very early breakfast of *xi fan,* which westerners refer to as a rice gruel—but it's hot, with a touch of salted pork on top, and it warms the body and the mind first thing on a cold Peking morning. Josh and I are becoming a familiar sight on campus, whether talking intently at breakfast or walking together between classes. And George, my boyfriend, fades from my interest. Now there's no one but Josh. Of course George, and C.T., and others do not disappear from my life—we're all friends, after all—but they're now backstage. Josh is the one I think about, on my mind nearly all the time.

Josh learns from others, and from me, that my grandfather, Liang Qichao (who actually gave me my name, *Nianci*), is very famous. This definitely piques his interest, and I make sure that he also knows that my grandfather found time to give me history lessons, when he wasn't busy with politics. And let's not forget how distinguished my father is too. I just want to impress my boyfriend!

Before settling in to teach law in Peking, my father, Zhou Guoxian, was the ambassador or "Consul General" to Burma, and the Philippines, and Canada. Our time in Canada is the reason I speak English perfectly. My father is a member of all the right clubs and associations in Peking (the non-colonial ones, the ones open to Chinese). He's a member of the Union Church, which reminds me: I know that Josh's name, Joshua, comes from the Bible. And ironically I know the Bible better than Josh does, because I'm a Presbyterian while he says he's not certain that there's even a God. His mother is a churchgoing Episcopalian but his father refuses to go to church, and so Josh (unlike me) was raised without religion. We both treat religion as one way to look at things, maybe an important way, but still only one way. Josh calls himself agnostic; I say I'm Presbyterian.

I learn that Josh has a huge appetite for adventure. Being with him is a wild gallop, not the orderly trot of a George, or the plod of a C.T. who's gotten too careful and serious since his arrest. Josh is an American, the only thing he's running away from is his family, and he knows no fear. He wants to see all of China, the China he's read about and seen in American magazines: Chinese shopkeepers and scholars in long gowns, the temples, the mountains, the pagodas, the Great Wall, the towering statues and the glowering monsters. Every temple has Buddhas, sometimes hundreds of Buddhas all tranquil amid this war. And there are statues of monsters everywhere, mostly guarding important places, of hideous grimace and bulging eye.

Josh has a Leica camera and he wants to take pictures of everything—rice paddies, water buffalo, peasants, temples, roadside shrines, the granite statues of the Ming tombs. We explore on bicycles, often going to the temples in the western hills beyond Peking. But we're mainly sticking to Peking, because no one can go far into the countryside without risking encounters with Japanese soldiers. Westerners like Josh can go more easily—the Japanese don't want to tangle with westerners, not just yet. So when I'm with Josh I feel safer, for now.

Besides, there's plenty to see in Peking. Josh thinks this city is exotic and as completely romantic as everything he's read about it. From the Yenching campus we go into the walled city of Peking by bus. For Josh, even a bus ride holds surprises, as I describe:

> *"The bus jerked to a stop to make way for a string of camels. They ambled through the archway in the street, big feet slapping against the smooth concrete, ugly faces passing so close to the open windows that people drew back with annoyance. Rickshaws and bicycles could still squeeze through, but buses could not. Bus after bus drew up to the side of the road. 'More than twenty,' an assistant driver shouted. The drivers shut off their engines. It takes quite awhile for twenty or*

*more camels to amble through an archway. Assistant
drivers fell out of their respective buses, in readiness
for the cranking. The passengers chatted pleasantly
in the cool dusk."*

Josh falls in love with the city I've always loved. I take him
through the snaking alleys (called *hutongs*) which are most of
the city's streets. Along the walled alleys are solid wooden gates
opening into dwellings that might be humble or might be
expansive, with multiple courtyards. The houses are single-story
with graceful tiled roofs, and cannot be seen from the street. We
visit my parents' large home and gardens, on a wide boulevard
called Dongzhimen Street, northeast of the Forbidden City.
There you enter through the solid, forbidding outer gate, then
step through a circular stone gateway called a moon gate, and
you find a courtyard and beautiful low buildings, roofs tiled and
turned up at the corners, the columns painted red. Inside, the
furniture is fine teak and *huanghuali* wood, though Josh finds
the chairs to be too low to be comfortable for his tall frame. But
he's too polite to complain, and besides he's enthralled with the
strangeness of it all.

Elsewhere in Peking we explore the markets, the open shops,
the air dense with noise and the spice smells of street food and
steaming noodle stands. As we wander along we stop to eat all
kinds of things entirely new to him. He loves it all. He's mastered
chopsticks and for snacks he's learned to eat salt-dried plums and
steamed buns filled with sweet bean paste. We go to the Chinese
opera, which Josh finds very strange, what with sawdust on
the floor and the audience busy eating and drinking while also
coming and going through the many hours of performance. The
actors in heavy makeup give out very shrill up-and-down singing
noises, and off-stage musicians thump their drums and produce

sudden alarming clangs from brassy instruments Josh has never seen before. The male actors wear masks and formidable boots while stomping and glaring and flashing broadswords. A bizarre stringed instrument whines constantly.

These are Josh's impressions, and when I hear them I lean back in laughter. He says, "I don't even like *Italian* operas, but at least they have some kind of tune, not just noises."

I just tell him he has a lot to learn.

And I make it my business to teach him all I can about China. Usually it's positive, all about our long and distinguished history, our incomparable culture and achievements, before westerners began to take over parts of cities and entire territories. Before Japan started doing the same thing. Before Japan attacked us. But there's the dark stuff of China too: warlords, opium dealers, criminals sometimes in gangs, and of course the dangerous secret police who work with the Japanese to put down unrest. And should things ever start to seem tame, I show him some of the items in the newspapers of Peking:

2 Beheaded in Peking

Disturbers of Peace Arrested A Few Days Ago Are Executed Near Temple of Heaven.

Two bad characters who were believed to have come to Peking to stir up disturbances were beheaded yesterday morning near the Temple of Heaven. One of them was caught a few days ago trying to set fire to property outside the Chien Men and confessed that he was one of fifty who were going to set fire to buildings so as to start riots...

This is the kind of thing that unsettles most westerners, like the occasional severed head displayed in a slatted box at the top of a traffic post, and sometimes entire hanging bodies strung up in parts of town away from the western legations. But Josh just wants to know more about how and why executions happen here, and how it's changed or not changed with the war. The thing about Josh is that he's game to learn more about *anything*. In the evenings we go to little restaurants and night markets. Just outside the East Gate to the campus is a small homey restaurant where courting couples often go to stretch out their cups of tea while getting to know each other. Especially in winter, it's a warm place that invites intimacy. We might spend an entire afternoon together there.

Deep in the markets one day, we push open the door to a store on Chun Shu Hutong with a sign reading "Silk Satins, Woolens, Sanitary Furs." A bell tinkles, a long-gowned merchant appears, and we're stifling our laughter about the word "sanitary." With fake solemnity and strikingly improved colloquial Chinese, Josh asks the shopkeeper what an *un*sanitary fur is all about, and then all three of us cut loose when the owner waves his arms and talks drama about bugs and grease and things that smell bad. Josh says he wants to buy me a "nice and *sanitary* fur," but the price is way beyond what he can afford. And besides, I already have a very warm fur coat that I never wear, not only because it's out of keeping with the times we're living in, but also because it was given to me by a slightly older suitor who wouldn't take it back when I protested.

Josh explores on his own and with others too. Before he and I had even met, he and his roommate rode their bikes to the base of the mountains at Nankou Pass, 60 miles round trip in a single day. Another time he went with two friends to the nightly dance at the Grand Hotel, but they overstayed and missed the last bus back to campus. So they found a cheap hotel, called the "Home Sweet Home," and for 73 cents the three of them rented a basement room for an overnight stay punctuated by footfalls because the basement stairs were actually located in their room. I burst out laughing when he tells me this tale. Laughter feels so good, because it makes me forget.

But there's no laughter when he tells me how he and another friend watched a Japanese "sham" attack on Peking, capped by an ominous Japanese parade on the main avenue in front of the Forbidden City. There was a scourge of crawling tanks followed by canopied military trucks with canvas sides tucked up to display grim warriors with machine guns. Only a month earlier, the Chinese troops had had their *own* parade, "10,000 soldiers" (they claimed) marching to their barracks near Yenching. But now Chinese soldiers are becoming scarce, maybe decamping to areas they think they can better defend, maybe trying to go home, some maybe joining the Communists. Every day, Japanese warplanes thunder over Peking, demonstrating enemy control of the skies. Now there's even a shipping strike, and the Japanese threaten to shut down this or that rail line, and you can't send letters to most Chinese cities nor to any places abroad. They're shutting down China, day by day bearing down on us. You see how we can never forget this war?

We still try to forget, and by doing western things too, such as going to Vetch's Bookstore to thumb through English-language books, and of course showing up for the dances at the Grand Hotel. Its fountains and terraces and graceful dance courtyard still attract a lot of western men (a few have brought scarce wives or girlfriends)—business types, diplomats, lawyers; English, American, German, French, Dutch, White Russians (Tsarist refugees), you name it. Don't forget that these are the countries with colonies in Asia, or doing major business in Asia, and all of them are alarmed by the Japanese invasion of China. Yet none of these countries comes to defend China. Instead these westerners, nearly all of them men, report on our activities, or travel around China protected by their foreign status. In cities they're pulled in seated comfort by sweating rickshaw men; or they shop ostentatiously, or they waltz in the courtyards of the fancier hotels. Or watch pretty girls, both Chinese and western. Or chase them. And they drink, sometimes to excess, claiming to miss their "womenfolk."

During this January of the new year we hear of a terrible murder. An English girl, about my age, is slaughtered and her body dumped at night near one of the major city gates, near the market place we go to so often, next to a hulking city tower. The girl, who'd lived with her father right across the narrow street from Edgar Snow and his wife, was unusually pretty. She'd lived in Peking all her life, completely fluent in Chinese. She knew these streets well because she rode her bike by day and by night, and she knew all there is to know about nighttime Peking, or so she thought. Rumor has it that she was murdered by Chinese gangs (the westerners like this theory), or Japanese soldiers (an inconvenient possibility for local collaborators or westerners wanting not to antagonize the Japanese military forces). Another theory is that she was murdered by western businessmen while courageously or foolishly resisting rape—also an inconvenient possibility for the western authorities wanting not to antagonize the Chinese by this ghoulish misbehavior. The Peking police are basically helpless to solve the case, because everyone has clammed up. And remember: everyone is more worried about a Japanese attack than they are about a pretty girl found disemboweled.

But *we* are worried, my friends and I. It shows that our daily life isn't safe any longer, even before the Japanese soldiers attack full-force. To most westerners, the streets of Peking don't seem safe—especially at night. There's spookiness in the unlit *hutong* streets and the long stretch of the Tartar Wall where bats stir at night in the towers. But we Chinese know our way around our own streets. I know how to get around in Peking by night—but so did this English girl! To think it might have been western men makes it especially frightening because I know so little about western men, whereas this girl did, she was a westerner herself and yet she was lured to a party by drunken western men and overpowered, so the story goes.

I think: Peking is disintegrating. It's cracking under the pressure. Westerners are cracking. My friends are fleeing. The Japanese army is tightening its grip everywhere around us, Japanese planes are filling the skies from the airfield they've just built right outside Peking. The local government is in cahoots with Japan, and has made itself blind to the petty cruelties by day and the violence by dark. The good westerners are leaving, while the bad ones—the profiteers and bullies and predators—are starting to run amok in this city. I fear: Peking will crack and it will be crushed.

CHAPTER 3

War Moves Closer

J osh had been planning to return to America in June 1937, after a year of study at Yenching. He's restless and has gone to a different college every year, starting at Harvard (which he disliked), then UCLA, and now Yenching University—perhaps to drive his parents nuts, his parents who were always frustrated because he'd go his own way no matter what they thought or said. He was their cherished oldest child. When he packed his bags for Peking, they could do nothing but stand aside, wringing their hands and later shipping him a trunkful of sweaters and other woolens for the harsh Peking winter. Josh's letters to his parents are few and short. During winter he sends them some photos he's taken, including (ever mischievous) a photo of the wall tower near where the English girl's body was found. He says nothing about it beyond jotting "Fox Tower" on the photo, nor does he mention the local lore about evil fox spirits.

I'm drawn to this man, this American who's full of adventure and who's fallen hard for my passion and my thinking and my stories. I've told him that my stories are about China, and about my family's contributions. My family, especially my well-known grandfather, worked ceaselessly to help create a strong China free of foreign domination. I think back to the first time I told Josh about my grandfather. It was a week or so after we'd met, and as we sat in the little restaurant at the East Gate to the campus, about to tackle our steaming bowls of noodles, Josh asked about him: "Your grandfather—he's famous, people are telling me. I know a bit, but what did he do exactly?"

I put down my chopsticks and sit back, pausing to collect my thoughts, thinking; now's my chance to impress.

"Well, there's a lot to say." Another pause. "His name was Liang Qichao, and he tried to reform the last Empire, the Qing Dynasty, because the Dynasty had let you westerners walk all over us, and it was ignorant about how to deal with the west, imperialism and colonialism and all that. Besides, the Qing Dynasty was not even really Chinese, they were Manchu, but that's just one aspect." (I didn't know whether Josh knew Chinese history).

"My grandfather wrote about all these issues in a news-paper he published which was read all over China, and his articles were about how important it was to reform the way China was being governed. This was 1896 or so, 40 years ago."

Josh nods, listening intently.

I go on, "You probably know about the Empress Dowager. She was a very cagey ruler for decades, but she was getting old and so she appointed her son to be her successor. But he died at age 18, so she appointed her nephew. When this new emperor turned 23, he asked my grandfather and another reformer, Kang Youwei, to advise him on improving the gov-ernment, because clearly something needed to be done about all these westerners forcing us to accept terrible treaty terms so they could keep on profiting from trading with China." My words keep tumbling out. "You know, the so-called China Trade should be called the *Opium* Trade, and it was forced onto us by England and America. They grabbed Hong Kong. Embarrassing and ridiculous because China had always been so strong before!" (my voice is rising, I pause).

"What happened with that new emperor?" Josh prodded.

"Besides Liang and Kang, he asked six others to come to the imperial court at the Forbidden City to provide advice. This young emperor then started issuing decrees right and left, trying to fix things, and he even made my grandfather's newspaper an official publication of his empire!" (I'm leaning forward, urgent).

"When the Empress Dowager got wind of all this, she cracked down. She locked up the young emperor in the Summer Palace and then she arrested all these advisers on the spot. Kang Youwei had already left the court for Hong Kong, and my grandfather Liang Qichao escaped to Japan of all places—isn't that ironic?"

I smile then and go on.

"At least one of the other advisors was forewarned, but he simply refused to escape. So all these six other advisers were taken by ox-cart to the main market place. They were told to kneel, all in a line, and then they were given some rice wine to drink. And then the executioner with the big sword cut off their heads one by one."

"My *God!*" Josh says. Then with amazement in his voice, "Your grandfather could have had his head chopped off."

"Yes, but he escaped to Japan. This was 1898, and even though Japan had already defeated Russia, it wasn't militaristic in the extreme way it is now. In Japan he could keep writing and publishing his political views, which upset the Empress Dowager, to say the least. She called Liang Qichao a criminal. By the way, in the history books, they refer to this whole event as 'the Hundred Days Reform' because it all happened so fast, a hundred days of reform and then off with your head." With my hand I mimic cutting across my neck.

"What happened then?" Josh asked.

"Complicated. First there was the Boxer Rebellion, but that's another story. It forced the Empress to try to reform, but it was too late for her. She died in 1908 and the Qing Dynasty pretty much collapsed by 1912. After that there were a few years of a new government, but the new president tried to make himself an emperor and then he died. Then the political system fell apart, into the hands of very powerful warlords. Most of China was ruled by warlords and some of them are still out there, though they might call themselves *generals,* in the Nationalist Army. *Ha.*"

I shake my head, pause, and then switch back to family. Josh is riveted.

"My mother is Liang Qichao's oldest child, and even though she was a girl she was always his favorite, because she was his first-born. Plus, he was only 20 years old when she was born, can you believe it, and it was *eight more years* before he had any more kids. So: she was special, he asked for her opinion on practically everything, and really she was his alter ego. He was determined that she marry the right person. You know, most of the older generation here still believe in arranged marriages, even today!"

I look at Josh slyly, to see what he has to say about this, but he just nods as though this is simply another piece of Chinese exotica.

"Anyway, my grandfather's old colleague, Kang Youwei— remember he escaped to Hong Kong when my grandfather escaped to Japan—he had an assistant or what-have-you, someone to help him do research and draft his speeches and make travel plans and so forth. This assistant of Kang's was my dad, Zhou Guoxian. When Liang Qichao met my dad and saw him at work and got to know him, he decided Zhou Guoxian was a perfect match for his oldest daughter, my mother, even though Zhou was ten years older than my mother. So my parents' marriage was an arranged one and it happened in 1914, and I came along a year later. End of story."

Frankly, I'm tired of this narrative by now. And I think Josh must be too, but it turns out I'm wrong. At every chance, he asks me about my family—where was my dad born, when did my grandfather Liang return to Peking from Japan, how did my dad become Consul General for China and in all those other countries, and so forth and so forth.

There is so much still to say! And while I'm not known to be bashful, I'm too modest to say how I hope that one day my political writings can do even half a justice to my grandfather's famous writings. Or at least not be an embarrassment. I too want to speak out to save China. He wanted to save China from weakness and misrule and humiliation by the west. I want to save China from Japan and all its cruelties to our people.

I tell Josh that actually it was Liang Qichao who gave me my name, writing to my mother to say that she should name me Nianci 念慈, which means "remembering compassion," maybe to honor his mother who'd recently died. I've been told this is a beautiful name, combining two characters of deep emotion: remembrance and compassion. This was my grandfather's gift to me. Remember I was his first grandchild, and he was only 42. Grandfather also suggested my nickname, Little Cinnamon, but I guard that name carefully, allowing only Huiyin (and later Josh) to use it.

"Obviously Grandfather was very interested in me, putting all this thought into naming me, because I was the very first of the next generation. In Chinese terms I was very special, supposedly." By now I feel myself blushing. This is all so Chinese, I think.

But all this family background impresses Josh beyond measure, and he now wants to be a scholar, a researcher, a teacher, an adventurer in ideas and in travel and in all things China. I start to see that we can have a truly exciting life together. We'll live in Peking, where Josh can teach and I can write, once the war ends. The world is big and full of possibilities for us. I'm in love! I tell only Huiyin and my two best friends at college, Anlin and Mary. Huiyin looks startled and her questions seem to carry a bit of doubt, but Anlin and Mary are full of happy commentary about this whirlwind love of mine.

A couple of weeks later, as Josh and I dodge rickshaws near the Tartar Wall, he grabs me by the waist, pulling me next to him as a bicycle swerves to avoid us. His arm tight around me, suddenly he blurts out that he wants to marry me. Marry! Do you *mean* that? *Escape the Japanese invasion,* he shouts to be heard, *by going to America.* I can scarcely imagine this, especially the part about marriage, and my first answer is stockstill stunned silence. Another rickshaw huffs by us. Then *yes. Yes!*

Our laughter is lost in the clatter of traffic. A man shouldering a long bamboo pole, weighed down at each end by heavy baskets of cabbages, nearly knocks me over when one of the baskets strikes me as he shuffles quickly by. A sidelong glance and I see a parrot take flight, escaped from its wooden cage, its blue-gowned owner's startled cry also lost in clatter. I'm *free.* I'll marry this American I've fallen for, and I'll escape.

BUT THEN MY PARENTS STOP US COLD, STONE COLD. THIS event I'm about to describe is terrible, it's cruel, it's something

I'll have to work hard to forget.

Here's what happened. After our happy decision, and without telling me, Josh writes a speech he wants to give to my parents. It's addressed to both of them, but he will be formally asking my father for my hand in marriage. This is how it is done in Boston, and he wants also to respect Chinese custom as much as he can, little as he knows about it. He rehearses his very respectful speech over and over with his roommate Gonglai, who coaches him on word choice and tones, so that he can try to get them right. He comes close. He tells me nothing about this.

A few days later, as we're walking to my parents' home on Dongzhimen Street, he surprises me by saying he's written out something he'd like to say to them, asking their permission for me to marry him. When we see them, he'd like to speak first.

What can I say? We'd already talked about my parents' wish that I enter an arranged marriage to a man from the right kind of family, just as my mother did, and her mother before her, *ad infinitum,* always tradition. *Men dang hu dui:* the families are well-matched in terms of social status, say the matchmakers. But *we* do not match, I remind him, and I say his plan will not work, no matter how sincere he is or how polished (or not) his spoken Chinese. We need to think of some other approach. Now we've stopped in the narrow street, and people are squeezing themselves past us as I stand there with my arms out for emphasis. Josh wavers not at all.

There's nothing I can do to stop him, short of canceling our visit altogether. I'm filled with trepidation. But I'm also swept away by his gallantry in reaching out to them. He is brave! Perhaps my parents will see his courageous effort, his sincerity, his goodness.

At the door my father shakes Josh's hand western style.

My mother, standing behind my father, merely nods grimly, and we all seat ourselves in the living room. They say nothing beyond the usual greeting for visitors, although my mother motions to a servant for tea service. Then clearing his throat, without even a glance to me, Josh wades right in by asking them, in carefully crafted Chinese, for my hand in marriage. The speech lasts maybe five minutes, maybe seven, maybe ten, I can't even remember. Josh's voice is steady even as he struggles for the right pronunciation. He keeps going. I'm almost crying with happy surprise because the speech is both heartfelt and suitably respectful, and not badly spoken. I clasp my hands before my face, as in prayer.

And then suddenly I see that my father's face has completely closed down, like window shutters abruptly snapped shut. His hand slams down hard, on the table. *"No"*, he says, in English. *"Absolutely not. Never!"* My father the diplomat offers not one more word. Far from helping Josh save face, he seems to want to crush him. Absolutely.

He and my mother both stand up and walk out of the room in utter silence. Even the servant, just setting out the tea, looks shocked. It is so humiliating, so cruel that I feel myself cringing, bending, as I quickly grab Josh's hand and we hasten to the door and out the gate, back onto the street like unwelcome peddlers. I'm sobbing now, I who never weeps, no matter what.

Josh is pale and shaken, and I have no words. On the street, we walk silently, his arm around my shoulders, public be damned, and his chin set at an odd angle. Up and down the alleys we go, huddled close, with shops on either side now lighting their night lanterns. When finally we speak, he tells me he wants to think about going home. Because it won't work this way, going first to my parents. He wants to persuade *his* parents that this marriage is right, and then he'll come right back to get me, marry me, take me away from danger, give me happiness. He wants to go home to America. But he's coming back, he promises.

This hits me in the stomach. I've gone from sheer giddiness about marrying my new-found love, to choked misery that my parents have hurt Josh so badly that now he wants to go home. Of course, with the big picture so threatening, no one has to stretch to see why Josh might want to quit China anyway, even aside from his humiliating failure to please my parents. The Imperial Japanese Army has stepped up the pressure on Peking still further. It's become impossible to tell whether some or all of the Chinese officials who govern Peking are part of Japan's plan to install collaborationist government once Japan has conquered Peking. And Josh hasn't forgotten that parade of coming horrors that he'd watched on Peking's main avenue, with Japanese soldiers driving rows of tanks and army trucks on *Chang An Jie,* the main street in front of the Forbidden City. More soldiers high-stepping their way after the trucks, followed by motorcycles painted in camouflage. The flag with the Rising Sun splayed around everywhere, red like blood.

I'd stayed away from this parade, couldn't bear to watch these invaders showing off their muscle so obscenely, while pretending not to be at war with China. It was a macabre charade, malignancy pretending to be ceremony. Japan hasn't started bombing Peking yet, but we know all about their war-planes and we hear them overhead. They're about to attack Peking, one way or another, by ground or by air.

I know all this is on Josh's mind.

He and I have talked about how top Japanese military leaders have probably been growing tired of the endless ground war in China and yes, after six years of warfare they're bogged down now, in the rice paddies, and their mighty General Tojo is growing impatient. Tojo's photo glowers down at us from the walls of most administrative offices, and in schoolhouses and stores, wherever people try to ingratiate themselves to the conqueror. There are at least a million Japanese troops in China by now, some say far more. Well over a million Japanese soldiers on Chinese soil! Meanwhile Japan has just signed an anti-communist treaty with Nazi Germany, which hints that the Japanese military forces could join with the Nazi forces.

Though he'd never admitted it, Josh had been worried that his parents wouldn't accept me. It probably hadn't occurred to him that it was *my* parents who'd be the more serious obstacle. He'd never be able to move them, not even an inch, before the walls closed in and the war arrived.

———————

THEN IN DECEMBER 1936 CHIANG KAI-SHEK, THE HEAD of the Nationalist Government, is kidnapped by Zhang Xueliang, the key warlord in northern China. The warlord demands that the Nationalists and the Communists stop fighting against one another and start forming a "united front" to fight Japan. After some back-and-forth, the Nationalists agree, and so the warlord frees the Nationalist leader. I'm giddy with delight:

> *"Chiang's free, I repeat to my poor, bewildered brain. That means an agreement. An agreement to defend China. He'll have to fight the Japanese now. No more energy wasted on our own so-called Reds. No more civil war. We're out to fight the Japanese. We have a*

clear leader. I begin laughing hysterically."

This United Front gives us heart, but it also means that open warfare with Japan is more likely. It won't be just Japanese soldiers skulking around with beatings and arrests and spying and torture. Now there's to be gunfire and artillery, planes revving up. The world is spinning toward a major war much faster than expected.

Here's what a map of China looks like in early 1937: you can see how the Japanese control Korea—they'd seized Korea over 25 years ago—and how they've now occupied Manchuria, in north China. Just south of the Japanese-controlled area is Peking; so we're squarely in their path as the Japanese soldiers move southward. South of Peking is territory still controlled by the Nationalist Government, and some places depicted as the "known" Communist areas—many Communist areas are unknown. And the rest of the land—a very large part of our land!—is ruled by warlords. The warlords are supposed to be under the control of the Nationalist Government, but most have minds of their own.

With nearly all the guns and tanks and planes in the hands of the Japanese Army marching ever southward, you can see that here in Peking we're just a big, fat, target.

So the quickening war is one reason why in February 1937 my beloved Joshua suddenly says he must go back to America. The humiliation heaped on him by my parents makes him think he can make no progress by staying here in Peking. And his parents have been telling him they'll cut off his funds for college unless he returns to the safety of America. His parents are consumed by worries, and he tells me why. The Japanese agreement with Nazi Germany has frightened them. One of Josh's younger brothers who's a student at college has decided to join the American Communist Party and do labor organizing. The Great Depression is rampaging across America, people out of work and forced to sell their homes and their household treasures, no money. In 1937 it seems the whole world, not just China, is coming apart.

Josh writes to one of his closest friends that his mind is at war with itself: "At one time, and I haven't yet despaired, my mind was made up to settle in Peking. When I'm not studying, and that's all the time, I hold lengthy debates on the subject, never getting anything decided, of course. So with one thing and another I feel now rather like the battlefield at Gettysburg." He's not given to overstatement.

It's a grim and wrenching goodbye for me. After we've climbed to the top of the high city wall, looking out over Peking's tiled rooftops at dusk, we talk again about the awful meeting with my parents, their stinging rejection of him because he's white, he's too young, he's from a family of merchants. I notice his voice is unsteady and his eyes a bit wet, but his hand is firm and his body close. So there's nowhere to hide when he leans still closer to tell me he's definitely decided to leave for America. Nowhere to go with my tears. "Little Cinnamon, *Baobei*," he says. "We'll be together, and it will never stop." But through watery eyes I see only nothing.

Gently Josh says that I have the protection of my well-known family with their contacts outside China, and I speak flawless English without even a trace of foreign accent, and I'm a fighter. All true. But let's face it, all bets are off if Japan seizes Peking and then goes on to Nanjing and Shanghai and eventually comes to rule all of China. That's the overwhelming fear. My family is powerless because they refuse to accept positions offered by Japan or by Chinese officials who bend to Japan's will. My father, my uncles, none of them will collaborate with the enemy.

It's dark now, and a bat swooshes by on its way to one of the towers on the wall. Below us, night lanterns are being lit everywhere. We need to get back to campus. Scrambling down the stairs, Josh hurriedly tells how he's been busy exploring how to get me to America ("to get out of this war"). He tells me his parents, these ramrod-straight Bostonians, are near speechless about this, so preposterous this seems to them. To them it's unimaginable that their first-born son has fallen in love with a Chinese girl.

They do not know, and he doesn't inform them, that our love has become close and urgent, frustrated by the shortness of our times alone together. We want more, a lifetime even. We've known each other barely two months, but already we know we must be together always. He's not yet told his parents that he wants to marry me, he says. He'll break it to them gently, in person, he says. And then he'll return for me.

BUT HOW CAN YOU TRUST WHAT PARENTS DO? THEY'RE hopelessly mired in tradition. After all, both of *my* parents had been perfectly polite when I first brought Josh home through the moon gate and into our family's courtyard. We drank tea on the main pavilion and exchanged pleasantries. My folks were plainly surprised that Josh could speak Chinese, and they were tactful enough to ignore his occasional mispronunciations and wrong tones. My parents were also pleased that Josh is so focused on learning about Chinese culture, and that he's so interested in my eminent grandfather. And having been ambassador to all those countries, my father's no slouch either, and both my parents know every diplomatic nicety in the book, not to mention history and international relations.

They know it all. My father is steeped in knowledge! And my mother, because she's Liang Qichao's first-born, is even more so. The conversation seemed to go well, mostly in English, so as not to tax Josh's Chinese language proficiency.

Yet I could tell from the flat straight line of my mother's mouth that she disapproved of Josh right off. Though they both try to hide it, my parents are not pleased to hear about Josh's family. Josh's father is a "merchant," according to my parents' way of thinking. He's in business, and not an impressive business. Josh's father is not interested in scholarship or world affairs. His main interest outside of business is a game called baseball. The family business used to involve cutting ice off of winter ponds in Massachusetts, then delivering the ice to provide the cooling for so-called iceboxes all over the Boston area. After the electric refrigerator was invented, the iceboxes were thrown out and the family business had to adapt. It started to provide heating oil for Boston households, as well as ice cubes for Boston drinks.

My parents are not impressed by this type of business. Their disdain is written all over their faces. They pretend to be interested so they can find out more, but the interest is fake and I can tell. After all, my father has dealt with Americans in much bigger businesses. He even owns stock in First National City Bank, with offices not far from our home; later it becomes Citibank. But to my parents this is all just merchant work, well beneath our family's accomplishments in diplomacy, political leadership, scholarship. None of that in the Bennett family; just plain business stuff.

Beyond the class differences, to my parents the central problem is that Josh isn't Chinese. He's a westerner, a white man completely beyond consideration for their only daughter. That became obvious to me only later, at that withering last meeting: the heavy hand of my father, slapping the table, the voice that barked *No!* And the cold, silent stare from my mother.

There had already been growing tension in our family between the older and younger generations, and in discussions around the table I tended to argue vehemently for our younger generation's right to do things differently. Sometimes I used words and ideas I'd learned from Huiyin. This annoyed my father and infuriated my mother. "You're just a student," she'd snap, and I should listen more and do as I'm told. She'd practically spit disdain, and I'd feel a terrible icy rejection of all my ideas. About my family, I write in hasty fury,

> *"Our older generation doesn't give us a chance to talk. They're always on the sharpest lookout for the slightest sign of disrespect, and they take every chance to fly into a temper thereby hoping to show general absolute power and all knowledge and all such absolutes. Purely traditional of course…I'm positive that the natural reaction of my 'oppressed generation' has always been the same. You don't know how terribly angry I get at times, ready to hurt almost, but somehow I never dare burst. Such an awful waste of energy on both sides, this never meeting on common ground.*
> *How can I even <u>think</u> of marrying a foreigner? But how can I even <u>think</u> of giving him up! I'm all pulled to pieces inside."*

Listen closely and I'll tell you that my father would have stopped the marriage, stopped it cold, whatever it took. He'd have cut off my funds, stopped the visa process, packed me off to Kunming or even farther away from Peking. He was powerful, he was connected, and when angry he was feared for the power he always held in check but which seemed to threaten utter destruction of those who crossed him. But next year—my father is *dead*. Let me tell you about that later.

With his death, my father's crushing rejection of Josh becomes vapor. So in the end I have only to deal with my mother. She carries with her my father's ill-will to match her own: dead-set against Josh, his race, his background, his upbringing, his family.

Of course, *Josh* thinks his family credentials are just fine. In Josh's family, they all went to Harvard (because it was the local college) and while they fought on both sides of their civil war, they were overwhelmingly on the Union side, "Boston Brahmins," so-called. I say to Josh: if you ask me, the American civil war sounds pretty tame compared with our warlords, bandits, peasant uprisings, heads chopped off and piled up like cannonballs on the ground. Compared to the Japanese invasion, your civil war sounds orderly and short, practically a tea party, only four years' duration and fewer than a million lives lost—whereas this Japanese invasion has brought nationwide chaos and government breakdown, it's been going on for over six years with no end even remotely visible, and already five million people have been killed, *most of them civilians*.

So his family credentials may be fine in America, but they come up short in China, in my parents' eyes. And there's no use saying his parents understand what China is going through, because nothing in American history even comes close to total invasion and civilian decimation by a foreign power. Their Civil War pales.

My friends and I debate this, and we see how Americans seem to live their lives in the same old place. Compared to

Chinese, they're complacent and comfortable. They're never driven out by powerful warlords, or invaders, or famine. They haven't had over a million foreign soldiers march into their country. They're very sheltered. This is what I say, and Josh sees it.

Was Josh's sheltered life the reason why he decided to leave Boston and seek adventure elsewhere, in China? With so much happening in the wide world, maybe Josh could not bear to stay put. The Depression was taking a deep hold on his family, and some of his uncles had been wiped out financially. America was on the move, poor families heading west, men sometimes riding the rails to find work elsewhere. And adventurous schoolboys looking for the romance of foreign shores.

At his boys' high school, Josh had been outspoken among his classmates. He read socialist writings and launched a student newspaper, *The Scholastic Proletarian,* filled with sarcastic humor about the school's rules and regulations, the stern teachers, and (importantly) deploring the rise of fascism in Nazi Germany. The schoolboys were afraid that war was about to break out in Europe (no one thought of Asia) and that America would get dragged into it, and all of them would be drafted into the army, rich and poor alike. Josh graduated from that boys' school as the intellectual rebel, the boy who disdained sports so that he could write his provocative political pieces—writings like mine!

After a year at college, which was just down the street from the family home, Josh decided it was too tame and that he needed to get away. No more family dinners at home. No more Harvard stuffiness. His roommate Willy, a fellow discontent from his boys' school, had flunked out after his first year. Josh watched Willy move on to the freethinking, freewheeling University of Chicago. So Josh decided to go even farther afield. How about China? He'd read about China in *Life* magazine and the *National Geographic*. He'd seen unspeakably beautiful photos of craggy mountains and painted temples, exotic pagodas and hardworking peasants bent down at work in rice paddies, those watery terraces jutting out of steep hillsides and punctuated by water buffalos.

He needed to get to China. But how? How to get his parents to go along with this? An idea: how about transferring to a university in the west? Such as Los Angeles. UCLA. California. And for his mother, Los Angeles was not so far from her Aunt Julia who'd married a rich man and lived childless in a mansion in Coronado. Josh humored his mother as she blithely assumed that Julia would be able to keep an eye on her rebellious son.

Off he went to UCLA for a year of study that also included many trips to the beach, the viewing of many movies, and the dating of at least one blonde. He saw *Top Hat* and was smitten with the movie star Ginger Rogers, but never learned to dance. He was only 18. He says he did go for a few weekends at his great-aunt Julia's in Coronado. It was a gloomy stucco mansion, styled Italian with terracotta roof tiles and vast corridors holding Renaissance art depicting plump angels. Not his taste at all. But Aunt Julia wrote reassuring letters to his mother, and that alone made the Coronado visits worthwhile.

Then suddenly (from their perspective) Josh announced to his folks that for his third year of college he wanted to go to Peking. You can imagine that his parents were shocked. You can also imagine that his mother was terrified, because the Japanese Army had been relentlessly making its way south from Manchuria, for the past five years, heading for Peking and aiming to conquer all of China. But his parents could no more control Josh than they could control the Japanese. Josh tried to calm them by telling them that Yenching University was headed by the well-known John Leighton Stuart, former missionary, widely praised in the American press. They were not comforted.

Josh was his own guide, and in 1936 he headed for Yenching. We didn't even meet till November! And by February 1937 as the flag with the red Rising Sun bled farther into China and the war animal menaced right outside Peking, he returned to America. Only two months together, but I was in his head and in his heart. In a way, Josh never left China.

CHAPTER 4

War Finally Strikes Peking

1937 is hell in China. Yes, the Nationalists and the Communists have finally come together for the time being, to fight the Japanese. But the Japanese have the war machines and the ruthlessness to use them on anyone in their way. Guns. Tanks. Artillery. Airplanes to strafe and bomb. Rather than risk further direct confrontation, the Nationalist Chinese Government is moving its capital from Nanjing, first to Wuhan and then to Chongqing (Chungking), much farther west and south. They don't want to fight the Japanese army in Nanjing. They take the Nationalist government deep into the interior of China, seeming to abandon the coastal big cities to Japan.

Then on the 7th of July, after six years of Japanese maneuvers and both organized and incidental attacks, the Second Sino-Japanese War officially breaks out. In China this war comes to be known as the Resistance War against Japan (though it had actually started in 1931 in Manchuria). At the Marco Polo Bridge (*Lugouqiao*) just outside Peking, Japanese soldiers and Nationalist soldiers begin open warfare, guns firing under the ferocious gaze of the stone lions lining the bridge. By the end of the month, in a move that didn't surprise any of us, the Imperial Japanese Army takes control of Peking, with hardly a further gunshot because the city's government simply packs up what it can and melts away. Those officials who stay are suspected of being collaborators. The Communists—the Red Army—continue their skirmishes against the Japanese, but they have almost no weapons. At every turn, the Japanese soldiers seize the weapons left behind by the retreating Nationalists.

Peking, historically the seat of Chinese power, has finally fallen to Japan. We're living in an occupied city with enemy soldiers no longer just lurking. They're now completely in charge. They are dangerous. Any Chinese man walking by a Japanese soldier on the street must bow or salute in passing. Women avoid walking alone, because these soldiers sometimes grab women they find attractive, sometimes in jest, sometimes in lust, sometimes in murderous rage. A stroll in broad daylight can turn into terror in an instant. By night it could be suicidal.

We close our doors to anyone we don't know. Yet we discover that some we know are collaborating with the enemy.

At Yenching we are shocked at the finality of this Japanese conquest of Peking, the thing we'd been fearing all along. We, especially the women students, are terrified about what might come next. The president of the University, that elegant John Leighton Stuart, tries to reassure faculty and students that because of its strong association with America, Yenching won't be attacked by Japanese troops. Nor will it be closed down, he says, unlike the other Chinese universities in Peking. The Japanese are bent on closing the universities, because they consider them potential hotbeds of anti-Japanese activity (they are right). Most universities—students and faculty, sometimes with books and equipment—flee to more remote areas of China, seeking to be beyond the reach of Japan. Naturally, Japan's hands-off policy on Yenching leads us to suspect that there are now more

Japanese sympathizers or outright collaborators within this university. A further pall descends upon us.

It becomes dangerous for anyone of importance to stay in Peking. Huiyin and Sicheng decide to leave Peking after Sicheng is approached by the Japanese rulers, who want him to start a "Chinese-Japanese Friendship Society" to help legitimize Japan's seizure of Peking. Rather than collaborate, Sicheng and Huiyin leave to go into the Chinese interior, eventually settling in Sichuan for the duration of the war.

Meanwhile we in Peking hunker down. We students try to study despite being surrounded by Japanese military rule—masked as a cooperative local government, but no one is fooled, and those Chinese collaborators, those puppets, are despised. Fears about Japanese-linked spies on campus rise to feverish heights. Your roommate perhaps? That history professor who avoids discussing Japan? You can't really trust anyone beyond your closest friends, and even then you have to wonder sometimes. C.T., for example, is talking openly about leaving campus to join the Communists in the caves of Yan'an, which probably means he was never a spy. Unless he's been recruited by the Japanese to spy on the Communists. You see how afraid we've become, how suspicious of even our closest friends?

C.T. keeps complaining about westerners. Now that Josh has gone back to America, C.T. presses me to forget about Josh. In a letter he hands me he calls westerners "arrogant functionaries and mere technicians who could never afford to live so well in their own countries," whereas "to support them in mansions with servants, we Chinese are enticed to rent land, build houses, plant gardens, pay taxes, all to these foreigners. Dogs and Chinese are banned from their parks." He's right. But in my mind I can only fight one war at a time. I'm fighting the Japanese invaders.

I'm still trying to write. In a way, it's become my life as I try to understand what's happening all around me. Over my college years here at Yenching, I've written so many articles that I've even been contacted by publishing agents in Shanghai and Boston. I've met with one who came to our campus. But out of fear of the Japanese powers and censorship, my writing has become more elliptical or metaphorical or otherwise devoted to descriptions of campus life, which I try to lift above the mundane.

On the front page of *World Youth,* published on January 2, 1937, before the official outbreak of war, there's a headline: *"Hold the Wall Against War in 1937!"* (note there's no explicit mention of Japanese invaders). Beside this headline is a photo of the Great Wall of China, and next to that a poem written by me. Here's an excerpt:

"THE GREAT WALL

There he stands
lonely and brooding,
hoary sentinel of an age-old country,
His weary arms
numbed
by years of resistance,
still
stretch bravely
across hill and plain,
ready
to defend his beloved China....

The old wall bared his sides,

feverishly absorbing heat and strength.

Great, gaping holes

like wide, toothless mouths

laughed at the beams dancing gaily

on the piles of sagging stones

the very vitals of the faithful guardian.

O, the power and the glory

that had once been his!

And all that is left

lies in mounds of crumbling brick

and grey dust.

But pride

is still in his bruised body,

pride unchanged and dignity unshaken.

With an air of supreme indifference

to all his failings

he maintains his majesty

and calm..."

And in the Department of the Mundane (but still heartfelt),
I write this in the Yenching University newspaper:

"In a sheer daze I passed between two stone lions and
entered my dream world. Chinese temples and palaces
set in southern-style-gardens—that was the 150-acre
campus. However, the thirty red-columned buildings

with tiled roofs and brilliantly painted undereaves
were thoroughly up-to-date in equipment; the gardens
included wide roads and athletic fields…"

From the Boston publisher I receive $4.00 for this worka-
day article, and I'm happy now to be a professional writer,
one who's paid.

Yet I cannot contain my voice, and it still sometimes
rushes forth:

> *"Everywhere there is a tense atmosphere of an ever-*
> *growing patriotic enthusiasm being constantly sup-*
> *pressed. Yenching is a haven of liberalism yet this*
> *very liberalism only accentuates the non-liberalism*
> *outside our walls.*
>
> *We who used to be content within these walls now*
> *realize that they do not enclose our actual world. This*
> *little world only serves to offer us a temporary gather-*
> *ing place where we may work with schoolmates from*
> *all parts of our country, not only preparing ourselves*
> *for future service, but shouldering right now our*
> *responsibility as young leaders in the immense task*
> *of national salvation."*

In writing this last piece I know I'm pushing to the
very sharp edge of what I can get away with: I'm calling for
national salvation. Still, strictly speaking, this is not explicitly
anti-Japanese or anti-collaborationist.

I no longer write my more strident anti-Japan articles. I'm
too afraid now, afraid I'll be arrested, or my family arrested
and tortured. We must be very careful now about these
Japanese, because now we're behind enemy lines, we're in an

occupied city, we're controlled by Japan. Peking is not flattened by Japan, probably because this city, with its Temple of Heaven and Forbidden City within, is the jewel in the crown of Chinese dynasties. No doubt Japan, if it prevails, wants to establish its Chinese seat of government in Peking, to rule China as most Chinese dynasties had since the beginning of time.

You don't mess with Japan, not if you're a "girl student" at a university that could be stripped to its foundations without warning by the most terrifying war machine in the world. Although students from more dangerous parts of China even now are trying to come to Yenching, most of my friends are desperate to escape. Many have already gone to Yan'an. Many flee to the south, to Nanjing or Shanghai, hoping to stay ahead of the Japanese scourge pushing south and crushing anyone in its way. Some of my friends apply to universities in America or Britain or France, these pillars of the west.

But then we learn that America won't allow any Chinese to immigrate. What! This comes as a surprise to us all. We'd thought the Americans were the very model of high ideals and welcome! Yet because of a longstanding law, America excludes the Chinese and *only* the Chinese. America gives many countries only a very limited immigration quota, but for China, alone among nations, it gives no quota at all.

We're shocked speechless. We scramble to solve this problem. I write to Josh. He says I can get around this for now by applying to go to a university in the United States, for a master's degree program. He suggests Wellesley College near Boston, because Wellesley has accepted Chinese students in the past, such as Soong Mei-ling who's married to Chiang Kai-shek. Soong Mei-ling, who persuaded Chiang to convert to Christianity, delighting the publisher of *Time* Magazine and other influential Americans. Josh tells me that Wellesley has a master's degree program in English language and literature, and it's even a "sister college" to Yenching.

But Wellesley is expensive, and in China our money has become worthless. I turn to my parents, but they are utterly opposed to my going to America, no doubt because they know it would allow me to be with Josh again. Obviously I can't possibly go unless I receive a scholarship, and so I apply for one. But Wellesley turns me down: it's too late for any scholarship money for the coming year. Would I consider applying for the year after that?

Of course I would. But that's over a year from now even to apply, two long years before I can leave. That's two more years under Japanese rule in Peking! Almost desperate now, I search for a job for next year, after I graduate, a job that will support me until I can leave for America. My parents have all but cut me off (but I'm getting ahead of myself), and I must get by somehow, until I can leave.

You ask: didn't Josh say he'd return to Peking to take you back with him to America? He did. But how could we know that war would be declared, official war, just four months after he returned to America? And that active war would mean Japanese bombers targeting almost all major strategically important cities? That flights and ships approaching China would be dodging Japanese sorties and that most would be canceled? Japan's goal was to cut China off from the outside world. To beat China into submission.

First they bomb Nanjing, in September 1937, just as I begin my senior year at Yenching. This bombing is fearsome, over 500 bombs dropped from the skies on people only trying to live their lives. They even bomb the main hospital. They want to bomb as many Chinese as they can, in the major cities, the cities they haven't been able to seize on the ground. They want to scare us into surrender. So now it's death from the air, the war screaming down on everyday people. They want to destroy our morale. Our fear cripples us. We feel useless, *meiyong*, but not hopeless. So Japan turns up the pressure.

In November their warplanes bomb Shanghai and thousands more are killed. We see—*everyone* sees—a photo of a Chinese baby, sitting strip-tattered on the floor of the burned-out carcass of the Shanghai train station, smoke and fallen steel all around, the baby bleeding from wounds all over, howling desolation, utterly alone amid the destruction. We are horrified; we want to grab that baby and run to safety. We've seen destruction on the ground, in the countryside and the cities, killing done by tanks and by soldiers aiming the latest modern weaponry at peasants and at city people. But until Nanjing and Shanghai we'd never seen killing from the skies. Bombing raids that shatter an entire city, no one ready for this.

Then in December comes an even more horrifying massacre in Nanjing, where Japanese soldiers unleash blood-soaked personal attacks, raping women at will, often killing them afterwards, executing men and bayoneting babies before their mothers' eyes. Over 250,000 people are killed this way. Over a quarter million people are slaughtered. The streets are soaked in innocent blood, naked bodies lying everywhere, out in the open, face-down and face-up. Eventually this massacre becomes known as "The Rape of Nanjing." But in the moment, as we read Chinese press accounts and we speak to those who have fled here from Nanjing, we turn almost to stone. Dread stone. How to deal with so much suffering, so much sorrow, so much cruelty that's actually enjoyed by the killers, killers in uniform? It's not enough to say that the

Imperial Japanese Army has run amok. They are a killing force across our land, they seek and destroy, they seek to lay waste all of China, they cannot be stopped because we have no arms to match their war machines, no murderous soldiers who would use machinery or bare hands this way, no savagery that would target babies.

I think: there is nothing to do but to run away from these killers, and nowhere to run to, except outside of China. I can't stay put because my name is on student writings against Japan, and that photo of our march against Japan shows me right in front. There are spies for Japan right here at my school. Each day there are fewer people I can trust. Each day there are people who ask me to join this or drop that. Each day more people are arrested, or just disappear, never heard from again.

Can I survive till the fall of 1939? Can I stand another year of this war? I stick to my books and keep my mouth shut. More than ever, I am very, very careful to follow all the rules, every single one. I just want to finish my senior year and get my degree and go to America somehow. To escape. To flee the terror closing in around me. And to be with Josh, whom I miss beyond all imagining. And I do imagine: I imagine our coming together again, nothing between us.

But I also imagine that he might be diverted by other possibilities, maybe a Ginger Rogers blonde, who knows. But how can he abandon me in the midst of such a savage war—and yet, how would he know how savage it's become here? He's in Chicago, safely studying and meeting old friends (Willy) and new. New friends. This only makes me more uncomfortable. I'm staggering under doubts and frightened by my own stare-eyed reflection in the mirror.

Returning to my dorm room one evening and closing the door—alone because my roommate has fled to her family in the south—I hear a small scraping sound as a note slides under the door. Scarcely glancing at the note I rush to open the door, and I spot C.T. heading toward the staircase.

"C.T.!"

Turning around, lopsided smile, he shrugs. Then he says in a voice barely above a hoarse whisper, "Come with me. Come to Yan'an."

"To Yan'an?" I'm not surprised at the destination, but I pretend to be, stalling for time.

"Yes. It's time to leave. Yan'an is where things are being organized to save China. Heilin has gone there, and Tommy too." These are friends of ours ever since our first year at Yenching, good friends whom we've worked with in our anti-Japan meetings.

"But where will I live if I go to Yan'an? There's nothing but caves up there." (Still stalling).

"In a cave. It will be an adventure. And I won't push you to love me again. We'll just be organizing to fight the Japanese, and that's a lot. We *must.*" His voice louder now, but still kept low to avoid any loose ears nearby. "It's time to take a stand and fight."

His words just hang there. Seconds go by. I'm a city girl. I'm a writer. I'm a fighter, but I fight with words. I want to escape to where I can do my kind of fighting, writing without fear of arrest and imprisonment. And I want to be with Josh! Which means America. I don't want to be with C.T. in a cave. I know he wants me back, and maybe his new commitment to the Communists is just a ploy to get me to run away with him. I almost laugh at the thought, I'm so nervous, but I also see that my spirit, my heart, tug me to do something completely radical, what C.T. is asking me to do. I'm starting to shudder. I can only look at the ground and shake my head.

C.T. lets out a long slow breath, then brusquely walks away and races down the steps, away into the night.

Back in my room I open his note: "Meet me at the island bridge at No Name Lake near the steps (you know where) tomorrow morning at 9. I have news."

I never see C.T. again, though years later I see his name, his new name, in the papers.

With C.T. and many of my friends gone to Yan'an or even to Manchuria or elsewhere, and in a panic to escape, believe it or not I actually write to Josh's *mother* to make sure that Josh still loves me. Josh has turned out to be a sparse correspondent, and I don't know whether this means lack of ardor, lack of time, or censored mail. So I ask his mother for information that will help in my relationship with Josh. Plus, I simply want her to like me. I don't know whether she'll tell Josh what I've written in my letters to her. But I have nothing to lose. To me, she and Josh's family are America, the America I need to reach. Please help, I say, but not exactly in those words. I just want her to see how human I am, how vulnerable, how worthy.

The English language is my secret weapon. I'm not like the Chinese she sees in Boston's Chinatown because I speak English as well as she does, in fact. Vocabulary and grammar are my special strength. But of course I let her see that for herself, in my letters. And that I'm worthy of her son, her first-born. I'm sensible, and I might even drive some sense into him, she might think. I'm desperate to escape the Japanese, but I don't actually say that because we're told our mail is censored by the Japanese authorities in Peking, and they keep a very close watch on us students. Maybe especially me, because of my pamphlets and the way I spoke out.

LET'S GO BACK A FEW MONTHS, BEFORE JOSH LEFT PEKING. When he first wrote to his parents about his feelings about me, they agonized that he was thinking about even *inviting* a Chinese girl to Cambridge, never mind *marrying* one. They hurriedly wrote to a Presbyterian missionary in Peking and asked the clergyman please to visit my parents and then to report back to them in Cambridge about what my Chinese family is like.

The missionary, a Mr. Gleysteen, who already knew my parents, duly came over for a visit. This visit was a cakewalk for my parents who are very used to dealing with foreigners, and they passed the missionary's test with ease. Like me, they know how to charm. To save face, they never mention Josh's proposal, although in their reticence some hostility may have shown. The missionary isn't stupid; he suspects deeper waters.

Gleysteen writes to Josh's parents to say that my family is an upright Christian family, Chinese indeed, but with good English and perfect social credentials as well as *church* credentials. When later told by his parents of the missionary's letter, Josh hoots and says that his mother can't complain any further (his father, not a churchgoer, is another matter). I don't have to point out to Josh that my father has been an ambassador to various countries, and if anyone knows how to handle official foreigners, that would be my father, for heaven's sake. Josh sees the joke, but his parents would not. They'd think about what the missionary says in his report about me:

> "Nancy is a charming young lady. She is very attractive, bright, and popular. I should say that she is the kind of girl who can marry almost any man she wishes. And I'm sure she would make an excellent wife."

But the missionary goes on:

> "While I agree that true love between members of
> different races is quite possible, ample time should
> be allowed to prove that this love is indestructible,
> especially because of its international and interracial
> aspect."

Members of Different Races. Interracial. Despite the encouraging letters from Josh, I know that these Gleysteen opinions are hanging over his parents' heads. They like what they hear about my family, but they don't like "interracial." So, as always, I take the bull by the horns and I write this to Josh's mother:

> *"This Mr. Gleysteen doesn't know what he's talking
> about. I won't make an excellent wife and Josh knows
> it. He will meet someone who will be much better for
> him, a nice American—at least, a white—girl whom
> he can marry without any trouble."*

This is straight out of the Chinese aspiring-to-be-daughter-in-law instruction manual. This is how you appeal to a future mother-in-law. You see, I'm showing Josh's mother that I care about her son more than I care about myself. I'm showing her that I'm not a grasping woman chasing her son. I'm not crazy, and I know perfectly well how difficult an "interracial" marriage can be. I'm worthy of her son. She must see it.

So starts my letter-writing campaign with Josh's mother. I write so well that these letters are often entertaining and sometimes even funny. I confide that my family is totally opposed to my hopes to spend my life with an American. I weave into my writings how Educated and Normal and Church-going my family is. I can make people smile, I can make them laugh. I can tell a story that lights up a whole room, or makes a 48-year old woman in Cambridge chuckle as she reads each letter from the Chinese Girl who has beguiled her son. I know she loves these letters, because she keeps them for the rest of her long life.

All of this is so Chinese. In China, a bride joins her husband's family and goes to work for her mother-in-law. It's your *mother-in-law* you must please, even more than your husband. So says Chinese tradition, the very tradition I'm rejecting in wanting to marry Josh. But this part of the tradition I'll use for my own purposes, because it works.

Josh's mother begins to sympathize with my plight. She begins to pay attention to the ghastly newspaper stories about the Japanese invasion of China. She'll understand why Josh is so worried about me. She goes to see *The Good Earth,* a movie that's all about the sufferings of the Noble Chinese Peasant, though without a single Asian actor in the movie. In reading *Time* magazine and the newspapers, she sees more and more pictures of the Chinese President and his stunning young Chinese Wife who graduated from Wellesley College. Now we're starting to get warm. Josh's mother may begin to see that I'm a lot like Soong Mei-ling: I'm Educated and Christian and speak perfect English even though I'm Chinese.

Of course, even if she tried to, there's nothing she can do about this Chinese girlfriend, if Josh wants to marry me. Josh has always gone his own way, and he's very good at ignoring his folks. His parents are staunch Republicans and have been known to rant against FDR and taxes and the New Deal. But Josh has always leaned left. He sometimes calls himself a Socialist but of course he isn't, he just likes to unsettle his folks, to Get Their Goat, he says. Maybe at first they thought he was teasing and tweaking them by snagging a Chinese girlfriend.

But soon they begin to see that he isn't going to stop trying to rescue me from this terrible war. His mother is the first to soften toward me. It takes his father many more years to accept me.

I enter my senior year at Yenching. I continue to make like the good girl I never was before. I pipe down. I study and see friends, but it isn't the same. I write about "locking away all my gay party things." Now I always wear the standard blue cotton gowns and black cotton stockings and rough shoes of everyday Peking. Josh's mother wants to send me some fancy angora gloves for Christmas, but I say please, no, nothing like that please. No purses or scarves or earrings. It's too hard here, life is too hard, we can't have fancy things when people are starving outside our campus walls.

———————

THEN COMES A SICKENING SHOCK. I LEARN SOMETHING that hurts me so deeply that for days I struggle just to breathe normally. I find out through a Chinese friend that Huiyin has written to an American friend about my relationship with Josh. In her letter, Huiyin says Josh isn't good enough for me, calling him "a white boy," a student without good background or a job, "comical" in his attempt to ask my father permission to marry me. She says my love is foolish, I'm only interested in Josh on the rebound (*what?*), and interracial (*that word again!*) marriage is wrong. And the killer is that she agrees with my parents in their refusal to allow this. She actually agrees with my mother, whom she's fought with ever since they met!

She gives details she could only have learned from me, because I'd shared with her my dreams, my nightmares, my humiliation about the meeting where my father flatly rejected Josh.

Huiyin! You encouraged my independence! You introduced us! How can you speak of Josh this way?

Huiyin! You've *never* agreed with my mother, everyone knows that, and you were the one I always went to when my mother was berating me for being too western.

Huiyin! *You're* the one who's explored the west, who's defied the old Chinese traditions in many ways. You're the one who led the way for me. No, don't tell me you've always hewed to the family no matter what, because I know it's not true. And now you tear down Josh to others, saying he looks like Shelley the poet and saying he's aimless—but what about your poet, who died in the plane crash? Because of that, you never even had to decide whether to commit to a different life. But I had to choose, and I made the commitment, and now you belittle me and attack Josh!

Sharp criticism and screaming hurt pouring forth from my heart—that's not me. But I don't know how else to deal with this. In fury I go to Qihua Men, an eastern gateway from the walled city, where Huiyin and I once rode Mongolian horses, and for a few *yuan* I mount one and head into the open fields and villages beyond, pounding hard and crying openly, fear of Japanese soldiers be damned, I don't care, I've just been betrayed by one of my closest friends, you can't hurt me more than *this* hurt. Riding aimlessly. A lost girl.

Then I see a lone warrior statue, a Chinese general, standing tall in a rice paddy, a sentry made of granite, with sword at rest. Calm. Vigilant. Surrounded by the very food of life: rice. Idiotic maybe, but this calms me down; my breath returns, I canter home. I write an anguished letter to Huiyin, and an angry letter to the American friend who's let others know how much my family opposes Josh, our plans for marriage now nearly stillborn.

But *I will press on, press on, press on,* even without my closest ally in the family.

I never speak to Huiyin again. I banish her from my life. The war makes it easy—she and Sicheng have fled Peking. But mainly it's because my stinging sense of betrayal tells me I cannot trust her again. Never. By wielding her mighty pen and starting gossip against Josh, she has hurt him and she has hurt me. Don't tell me she didn't mean to.

THE STREETS OF PEKING ARE FILLING WITH MORE AND MORE refugees from the Japanese attacks; the refugees are penniless, maimed, starving and begging on the streets everywhere, mouths agape with despair. The literate ones write their stories in chalk, on the sidewalk, and sit beside their stories, hoping for a few *yuan* tossed into their tin cups. The westerners can't read the calligraphy sidewalk stories, and they give nothing. The westerners have been leaving Peking in large numbers ever since the Japanese occupation, taking the train to Tianjin to find passage on ships leaving China. We students become very quiet. Caution thrown earlier to the winds has turned into risk come back to haunt. People disappear at night. We look over our shoulders. I write to Josh:

> *"This winter is going to be hard, so it will be hardest on the weak ones. Outside campus walls, every night almost, robberies are committed. In the hills the bandits loot on much larger scale. But they <u>have</u> to. With the cold weather, already scarce food will only get more expensive. The poor are in a terrible plight, really terrible. Relief work will have to be*

carried on a tremendous scale, yet that can't prevent
small babies and weak children and old people from
famishing and freezing. Late at night, we can hear
the gunshots close by, as distant cannon in the hills,
see searchlights sweep the sky as an airplane roars by.
Most of the time I cry when I am too battered by fear,
I spend the night making resolutions—anything to
get out of this...Never can I get rid of the feeling of
uselessness..."

"Uselessness", *meiyong,* the word we all use often. The word says we're powerless, trapped, fearful, unable to push back on the forces surrounding us, the tight grip of the enemy strangling our city.

COMES THE IMPOSSIBLE: MY FATHER'S GONE. HE'S KILLED by a group of Japanese soldiers. The papers say it was a bicycle accident, but the truth is that while riding his bike on his usual route to work, he passed new Japanese sentries without saluting them. He was called to halt but still refused to salute. So they pushed him to the ground. They smashed his head on the curb. He never regained consciousness, dying two days later in the hospital.

For his defiance, my father paid with his life.

I feel guilt—horrible, corrosive, eating my insides. My last words to my father, just days ago, had been hurled in anger and hurt. *You've no right to rule me, to tell me I can't marry Josh, to threaten me this way!* And words much, much worse, terrible words he'd never heard before from his daughter. I flung them out because he was threatening to freeze me out of school, not pay for my last term so I'd be denied my college degree when I was so close to graduation. He'd just stood there, arms folded, implacable, no give at all. So I slammed out of the room, my fury a monster unleashed and now forever loose in my recall, needing to be gripped, held down as guilt, guilt that never goes away. It's my birthday. I'll never celebrate it again, because it's the day the monster returns.

I never speak of my father again, unless asked, and even then I say almost nothing. No one in my future will know my father.

White chrysanthemums pile high at the Peking Union Church, which is filled with shocked associates, friends, and family. Dignitaries come to pay their respects. Strangers come. My father had spent over 20 years in Chinese government as a diplomat before becoming a professor, and he'd stubbornly turned away offers of positions in the puppet government, refusing to collaborate. I hear whispers that he was targeted by the Japanese, killed as an example of what happens if you refuse to bend to Japanese rule. Some say he was one of the local leaders of opposition to Japan, and I recall those quiet evening visits by various unnamed men and colleagues. Maybe this is one reason for the astonishing outpouring of public sentiment about his death, all those people paying their respects at his casket.

My mother is now a grim cipher. Always strict and humorless, at 45 she's suddenly a widow, and she rises to public occasion with a dignity and stoicism learned from birth. But her private face to me is completely locked down. No tears, no words, not an embrace, nor even the smallest touch, in our shared loss. To her I've violated the sanctity of the family. I've brought dishonor to my ancestors. I've dishonored my own father, and my eminent grandfather. And now this—*this* is the price for my disobedience: my father is dead. She turns her back on me, pure ice.

In her fight with me about Josh, my mother had counted on my father's refusal to allow me to marry a *waiguoren* (foreigner). Now my father's gone, and with him a father's authority. Now she seems to hate me, plain and simple. I write, "things are horribly twisted somewhere. She is in a locked-and-barred state. I can't find any crack by which to enter." My mother still believes in a marriage arranged by parents. A marriage to a suitable Chinese man. An engagement formally presented to the ancestors before the wedding date is set: the whole tiresome ritual dictated by tradition. Hopeless! So I must give up on my mother. I leave her to my three brothers. Now she finds out that I do what I want. I'm *lihai*, fierce. Just like my father.

It seems everyone I know is leaving Peking, escaping Japanese rule. Their army or the local secret police censor our letters. We use oblique metaphors (such as the weather— "heavy rain today") to describe the toughness of their rule. We trust almost no one. Most of my close friends have left for other cities or other countries, or have gone to Yan'an or Chongqing. They are making choices under duress. Some will rise high in the People's Republic of China. Others will rise high in the Republic of China, Taiwan.

But I stay in Peking, because staying here is my best chance to reach America. After graduation from Yenching, I know I must support myself while I search for ways to get to America. It's only a month since my father's death, and I'm still numb, but I force myself to push on, the way he always did. I talk my way into a job teaching English to incoming students at Yenching, where I think I can be protected by the American college president and the few remaining American faculty here. But Yenching is not the same:

"All the familiar places, places I never go now. All the familiar activities. Young people actually lived here once—studying, playing, laughing. But now—Japanese soldiers sleeping in the libraries, the gymnasiums; refuse in the lotus ponds; wild grass in the courtyards; guerrilla bands roaming the hills; and in the city, refugees by the thousands, groaning, dying."

A friend writes from Kunming, in the south:

"We looked up and saw nine big bombing planes flying over our heads. They were beautiful planes (1938 American model!), flying in perfect formation, with red suns painted under their wings. So they are Japanese bombers! My blood was boiling inside…"

In a story that I write, a young woman worries that her husband has been tempted into collaboration, with all its dangers:

"He's a banker, and the family is richer than ever before. Rich. Illustrious. But I pleaded. I wept. I laid his infant son at his feet. His mother ranted and cursed until she, too, fell on her knees. What kind of upside-down world is this when a mother kowtows to her own son?

'It is too late,' he said. 'The Japanese will kill me if I refuse now.'

I replied, 'But others will kill you if you don't. Every day traitors are poisoned, stabbed, drowned in their baths by their servants.'

But it was useless."

My darkest hours are the ones spent wondering who in Peking I can trust. Fearing the Japanese, fearing their often hidden collaborators, I start to buckle. Though I'd said no to C.T. when he'd invited me to go with him to Yan'an to join with the guerrillas fighting the Japanese (was that really only a year ago?), now I'm toying with doing just that. With friends I sometimes go far into the Western Hills, supposedly to visit temples or to ride horses, but actually we sometimes meet with classmates who have joined with the Communists. Mainly these students are functioning as facilitators in some of the conversations with the Nationalists, but their main hope is to talk with "the West," to use their English to help persuade the western powers to come to the aid of China. We spread out on stone ruins, or in the grass, breaking out *bao bing* flatbread and candied jujubes, chomping and chewing over almost any idea, in our desperation to fight back against the invaders.

C.T. himself isn't there—he's changed his name and moved up fast in Yan'an, no time for picnics. And again I decide no, this isn't the way for me. I can't see myself giving up Josh—or taking up arms. Only my pen.

So I redouble my efforts to reach America. I keep a low profile while writing to Wellesley and other American colleges suggested by Josh, begging for admission to a master's degree program, and—so important—the financial assistance to make it possible. My American friends here pitch in, and in all my flailing about, they even manage to make me laugh. One evening we all play a game, making jokes about the college applications I've been sending out, and the recommendations I've had to drum up. It's a rare, rare evening of laughter and good fun.

One faculty friend pretends to write to Wellesley College, tongue in cheek:

"Whether holding conferences with freshmen—who are as bewildered by her charm as by their ignorance—or wending her way to a table in a crowded nightclub, Miss Zhou is a complete success. No more slender figure ever pushed its determined way onto a crowded Yenching bus. No more generous spirit has ever brought its owner during meetings to sacrifice a chair for a seat on the floor…these superlative qualities are equaled only by her ability as an instructor in the English language, where she consistently makes use of 'idiom' as an explanation for any and all grammatical peculiarities…"

Not to be outdone, another says,

"I recommend Miss Nancy Zhou as a candidate for any or every scholarship which your discriminating college is in the habit of giving away to deserving young women of far Cathay …Miss Zhou is deservedly considered an accomplished dancer and could hold her ground in any nightclub or dance hall. I need hardly say that her standing with men competent to judge her unusual qualities is unchallenged."

Next an American professor provides mock *gravitas:*

"There comes a time in the experience of the most hardened and hypocritical composer of adulatory effusions when, after penning innumerable painful and ponderous periphrases on behalf of unworthy postulants for scholarships, a thrilling opportunity presents itself to spot a new star. Miss Zhou is the most irrepressible and versatile student I have ever known. She has always cut the maximum number of classes and the best figures on the ice, she has never annoyed her instructors by handing in essays before they were due. She is the best skater, dancer, pianist, student, teacher and friend I have ever known. She is all there, always there, and never in the way."

We—my Chinese friends and I—are now laughing uncontrollably, as we never laugh these days. We've been steeped in worry, sometimes sodden with fear. We're clueless about how to win a place in a college in America. We're always looking for ideas on how to "look good" in the eyes of these faraway and fussy Americans who read our applications. Now we're helplessly melting into laughter, roaring and shouting about the absurdity, the strangeness, no matter the need to succeed. Our American friends can mock their system, because for them it isn't a matter of life and death. Yet we're swept along by their good cheer and their willingness to poke fun at these peculiar American ways. It's turning into a night to remember.

Finally the American professor, standing tall while raising a cup of rice wine, proposes a toast and solemnly intones: *"I write to importune you to give favorable consideration to the application of Miss Zhou Nianci—Nancy to you—for a scholarship in your institution of higher learning."* A mock bow to higher learning. More laughter, more toasts, more rice wine, and we all head home in the gathering darkness.

Nearby some planes take off, Japanese warplanes, destinations unknown.

THEN DELIVERANCE! WELLESLEY ACCEPTS MY APPLICATION and gives me the scholarship funding I absolutely need in order to go to America. Clutching the admission and scholarship papers, along with letters from some American friends of my family, I travel by train to Shanghai, to the American consulate. I'm wearing a simple cotton *qipao*, its high collar demure and sensible. My shortened and curled hair has been given a fresh styling that I hope will look earnest and studious to the visa authorities. In the sweltering rail car to Shanghai, I have to stand much of the way, crowded in with both Chinese and foreign refugees heading south. I mark this as the first step in a very long journey to come.

In Shanghai, the American consular official riffles through my papers, asks me questions about the Wellesley master's degree program, and finally issues me one of the hard-to-get visas for a Chinese person, strictly to study at Wellesley. He leaves blank the termination date of the visa. Perhaps he winked when he did this. I pretend not to notice. Maybe his receptiveness is because my English has no foreign accent. He thinks I'm not bad, not problematic, not the "yellow peril" that drove the Chinese Exclusion Act. Or maybe it's just the effect of *The Good Earth* and the Noble Chinese Peasant. I think this is a bit comical, but I don't mind taking advantage of *The Good Earth*'s heartrending tale of hard luck that makes people think the Chinese are wonderful and simple. Simple like a fox.

I return to Yenching. Now with my hard-won visa and my scholarship letter, I'm finally able to leave Peking and go to America. The year is 1939. The Imperial Japanese Army has pushed its way deep into China, and hopes next to conquer

Indochina (Vietnam) which is still held by the French. Japanese warplanes continue their bombing, striking Guangzhou and then Chongqing. Over and over and over and over again, those bombers hit Chongqing, now the seat of the Nationalist government. One long raid on a June day in 1939 kills 5,000 people in Chongqing, and I have no way of knowing whether my friends who'd fled to that city have survived. The Communist troops, the Red Army, are still based in Yan'an but they're organizing and growing in number in rural areas throughout much of China. The western powers refuse to help fight the Japanese. America stands back, far more worried about Poland and the Netherlands than about China.

In occupied Peking, I can't bear the thought of another winter ahead, when harsh gusts will cut down rag-clad refugees goaded by war, either herded or ignored by men in darkest blue answering to Japanese bosses. Another winter, and again people will slump, die in the fine yellow dust blown from the Gobi Desert, bodies buried by dust, shapeless mounds everywhere. Another winter, with Peking growing blurred and muffled and deeply secretive. Another winter, like the last one, when a Japanese soldier in goggles rode by on a motorcycle, sidecar bristling with a mounted machine gun. He swerved to avoid a dusty corpse lying in the road, the motorcycle roaring up the street and around a corner. That time I ran, ducking into deep doorways whenever I heard more motors.

It's a dangerous, desperate time in China. I cannot give up this chance to escape the Japanese, and here it's arrived. I go despite leaving behind my mother. She's locked me out of her life, completely, for falling in love with a westerner. She doesn't want to leave China, or even Peking, unlike two of my brothers who have moved inland. She's Chinese, China's seen plenty of political upheavals, and she trusts she'll survive the

Japanese army by simply keeping a low profile and by staying where she is in Peking (she turns out to be right).

In times of war and terror, families break up. People leave their homelands. The Japanese invasion and fear of arrest for my past political activities drive me away from China. It's not forever. Never once did I think it would be forever—because I'm going to return to China, no matter how long it takes to defeat the Japanese. With my husband I'll work in America to help Americans see that they *must* help China defeat Japan. I'll write articles. I'll make connections. I'll work like a demon.

After all, I am Nianci. I am Remembrance and Compassion, named by my grandfather Liang Qichao. In time, I learn that over 20 million Chinese died because of the Japanese invasion of 1931-1945, the vast majority civilians, from killing and starvation and relentless bombing, death from the sky, people collapsing while fleeing on muddy roads, rampant disease unleashed by destruction and desperate flight, entire villages torched and bodies left to waste under circling vultures. This number of deaths is beyond comprehension, and I do not forget. Even when I do not speak of it.

I do not forget.

When this war is won, and I know we will win because we *must*, I'll come back with Josh. He'll teach at Yenching, and maybe I will too, and we'll raise our kids in Peking, surrounded by family.

This is my vision, my dream. Our vision, our dream.

CHAPTER 5

War Upon War

W.H. Auden, from *Journey to a War*, about his trip to China during the Japanese invasion (written in 1939 after his return to safety):

Here war is harmless like a monument:
A telephone is talking to a man;
Flags on a map declare that troops were sent;
A boy brings milk in bowls. There is a plan
For living men in terror of their lives,
Who thirst at nine who were to thirst at noon,
Who can be lost and are, who miss their wives
And, unlike an idea, can die too soon.
Yet ideas can be true, although men die:
For we have seen myriad faces
Ecstatic from one lie,
And maps can really point to places
Where life is evil now.
Nanking. Dachau.

SUMMER, 1939. I SAIL BY WARTIME RAMSHACKLE STEAMSHIP to Seattle, on deck the salt wind blowing away my war fears as I head toward America where Auden says war is still harmless, where evil is not aloose across the land. In Seattle, I find my way to the train station to continue my journey to Boston. I sneak up to the parlor car of the train and I look out on a vast country untouched by the wars raging in Europe and Asia. I think: can this be true?

> "'Be careful,' pleaded Old Woman.
> 'No,' the girl replied. 'Never again will I be careful. There are worse ways to leave this earth than to ride into a wind of my own making.'
> 'How inauspicious, the way you talk.'
> 'Come, Old Woman, how often have I fallen off a horse?'
> Take a rock mountain, sterile, bare. Touch with green, enliven with creatures. Lions yawn at gentle deer leaping. Here stalked ancient archers. Here whooped emperors long dead. And here am I, on my winged horse, never to touch earth if I so wish.
> All this I would gather to myself, and in greed, more. I will search the topmost branch for a slender dragon, part the moss and fern to find an infant phoenix. Wings of rainbow bats will brush across my brow. Fireflies will light my shadows.
> The horse galloped swift and sure, hooves on the firm brown earth. Short hair flung loose, light clothes in billows, the girl on her horse ripped into the summer forest, slitting the wind in two with her face."

I'm on my way. I say I'm not superstitious, but I need lucky now. So I gather all the luck I can—the dragon, the phoenix, the bats—to find a new life. I leave behind my whole family, but still it's auspicious. And then I say to myself, *Stop! Stop* being so old-way Chinese! I'm doing the new way. Now that I've made my decision, I *must* do the new way. I force myself to hope. And I gallop.

Josh meets me at the Back Bay Station in Boston. A startled wave of his arm when he first sees me. Then our deep embrace is as though he'd left just the other day, not two-plus years ago. Men in seersucker or linen suits charge past us looking important with their fedoras and briefcases, as the steam roiling from the train reaches to envelope us all. Finally we break away and Josh drives me over the river to Cambridge to meet his parents.

His parents, like mine, are initially cordial. His father, tall and lumbering, doesn't say much, and he harrumphs often, almost but not quite impolite. His mother is exquisite: a delicate beauty with silver-blonde hair pinned back with a clasp, and a soft silk dress that I want to think she chose specially for this occasion. She is carefully friendly. As we enter the living room and she fusses with some flower arrangements, she mentions some of my letters, the ones about the gifts I'd like to bring them. We sit down to dinner in their dining room, which is comfortable but not large. In fact the entire house is not large, compared to the houses I've lived in. And the food is terrible: bland, boiled, boring. But of course I'm too polite to show disappointment about anything. And I want, very badly, to please Josh's parents.

Like all Americans, they're amazed that I speak English as well as I do. I'm as charming as I can possibly be, which is very charming. I smile, I tell them all about my family, but I leave out the anguish, and choose stories that I make funny, poignant, captivating. Possibly they think I'm a dollish curiosity, a mannequin, but actually I can see Josh's mother chuckling and enjoying my company. She sees me as a person—a dark-skinned person wearing a form-fitting high-collared Chinese dress—but definitely a person not so unlike herself had she not married such a gruff, big, taciturn man as Josh's father. She's prepared a guest room for me in their house. But I cannot stay there long, because it feels to me like an imposition on people who haven't yet accepted me. And besides, there's no privacy possible, and Josh and I have hungered for each other for so long.

So Josh rents me a room in a small rooming house on Story Street in Cambridge. I like the address because I'm now writing my own Story, free of my forbidding mother and safe from the Japanese army. And because in my small room there, Josh and I can discover one another for the first time since Peking.

I dive into learning about this new country, this land of freedom from terror. No Japanese sentries posted on main streets nor suddenly on side streets. No hoarding of rice and cabbages in case of hunger. No one dead on the street at dawn. Instead, at dawn here the streets bustle with people in a hurry. At noon they're shopping or lingering relaxed in the parks. The street noise is mostly vehicles motoring and braking. No yelling vendors or huffing rickshaw men or camels or donkeys or noodle stands. Even the pigeons are different, as I write while sitting in a park:

"It is usually full of pigeons. The strangest pigeons. They never seem to fly up into the sky the way they do at home. They don't wear wooden whistles under their

tails either, but then nobody bothers to steal them, so why should they wear whistles. They just hop around on the ground and eat."

And coming from a country where memorials to the dead are revered, I learn that Americans revere them differently:

"The architecture of [Harvard] is most mysterious, especially the Memorial Hall, but people seem to think it so good that they put it on plates so they can look at it while eating. Boiled potatoes and boiled spinach served on Memorial Hall is, well, the other guests don't consider it an insult, so why should I?"

I'm surrounded by white faces, some of them looking at me with curiosity because of my dress or my not-white skin, but in Cambridge they're generally used to Chinese students here and there:

"There isn't much we can do except interpret the situation to people. Frankly I think we bore them. They don't even know that America is sending Japan the gasoline and metals they use to bomb China, so what is the point of telling them it's all wrong? 'Representatives of China' we students are called..."

Then to Wellesley in the fall. After all the political pressures and dangerous intrigue of Yenching, Wellesley is a burst of freedom. Because I've gone to such demanding schools, the course work and writing for the master's degree are easy enough for me, though of course I have to figure out what the instructors are looking for. I'm surrounded by white American girls, but (like most) they're full of curiosity about someone from so far away, and who's had all the adventures I've had in my life. At Sunday teas, I try to impress them by telling them about Peking, and about the usual story of my eminent grandfather escaping beheading by the Empress of China and so forth. In America, my account eventually becomes practically a canned speech. But the story is *true*. It's where and what I come from. I want to make sure that people know that I'm proud to be Chinese.

About the tea itself, nicely served with dainty pastries each Sunday in the vast living room of the dorm, I can only cringe, silently:

> *"Of better teas, practically all of the young green tea, the best, was kept for drinking in China. Of the lower grade, red or smoky, the choice was kept in China for the cooking of eggs; the inferior was sold to England and America for wasting with milk and lemon and sugar..."*

And so at Wellesley I learn to drink this tea "black", while pining for the green tea of home. But this is minor. What's major is the contrast between the order and safety of Wellesley campus life and the seething, shape-shifting pressures of Yenching campus life. Where Peking was terror without process, here there's plenty of process, no terror:

> *"You would be interested in the Student Government of this great women's college. I was invited to a trial. Of the two matters taken up, one concerned a girl who was seen smoking while walking on the campus. Was she guilty or not guilty, and so on. It took half an*

hour. The other matter was a very complicated affair about whether or not a girl was lying when she said her thirteen-year-old brother was a chaperone. It was just a matter of principle. The Student Government also decides on the color of the corsages worn by usherettes at campus balls and such."

I return to writing things for publication, but this time they're not political. They're vignettes and painterly writings about life in "old Peking," the traditions. *Wellesley Magazine* publishes one of my pieces, about courtship and arranged marriages in old China. In my article I don't support these practices, but neither do I attack them. I know that my description sounds tame, as I leave out my strong feeling that arranged marriage is unfair to women. Especially when men could have concubines! And wives who fail to bear a son must move over and make room for a concubine. Awful. But I don't want to put off these American readers by delving into practices they find bizarre—although as I write, I feel fiercely Chinese, very different from the readers of this magazine. Yet I'm not old China. I'm new China, and I let everyone know that.

So America is safe, and Wellesley itself is having a romance with Yenching University, its "sister college." In the November 1939 *Wellesley News*, I see this piece:

"Yenching is needed to keep alive the 'liberal arts' spirit and high type of education it has been able to offer to the young people of China. War conditions in China have increased the financial needs of the University appreciably. Many of the students have lost parents, homes, and fortunes, but they still fight on to gain an education. An education may indeed be the only weapon they will have to maintain any kind of stability in the situation they find themselves today. Some students have come on foot distances equal to that of Kansas to New York, in order to attend Yenching. Many other universities have been destroyed, driven out, or brought under the domination of alien conquerors."

I notice that they do not say Japan; they say Alien Conquerors. They do not say Invasion; they say Situation. *Why do Americans pussyfoot around what Japan is doing, what Germany is doing? What horror would it take to get America to respond to mass killing?*

During my Wellesley year, Josh is in Chicago. He'd headed there after he left Yenching, wanting to continue pursuing his interest in China—yet away from his parents. The University of Chicago has more than a few Chinese students; he'd met some of them at Yenching. Chicago isn't Yenching, of course, but he's gotten his bachelor's degree and is now working hard on a PhD in Chinese history. I'm proud to see he's getting excellent grades—my choice of partner is justified! Josh is more interested than ever before in learning everything he can about China. He hopes to return to Yenching University as a teacher, after he receives his PhD several years from now. His eyes are always on China.

He comes to Boston to visit me at Wellesley, and sometimes we drive to the New Hampshire mountains where his family has some land. We walk the land. We picnic. We lie in the grass together. We walk around a dilapidated old apple orchard, long neglected in these mountains. We find the stone foundation of the abandoned farmhouse where the apple farmers used to live. I take a photo of Josh standing rakish, his head cocked to the side, leaning against the stone foundation. He takes a picture of me with my hair in long pigtails for our climb, wearing a very American flannel shirt and dungarees, no slithery Chinese dress but a statement nonetheless. A commitment. We know we need to be with each other forever.

When I finish my master's degree at Wellesley in 1940, Josh and I decide we're tired of waiting for everyone's acceptance of us. It's time to get married. *Kexi kehe!* Time to celebrate! I write a long letter to my mother, in what I hope is a conciliatory tone, but she does not respond. Perhaps my letter never reached her in wartime Peking. Perhaps she's boycotting the wedding and too angry to say so. I'll never know. But I work hard to make the wedding not just American but also Chinese. For my silver pattern (yes, silver!) I ask for engraving with the Chinese characters for my name, 念慈。Of course the jeweler has a terrible time trying to engrave this onto the silver, but the cutlery still looks beautiful. I tell everyone that it's unlike anything they've ever done before in America. I'm never bashful about accomplishments.

Though Josh's mother may even be pleased about the wedding—she doesn't actually say it—his father is only resigned. When the *New York Times* calls him to confirm that his (actually not) Harvard-Educated Son is indeed about to marry a Chinese Girl with an unpronounceable name (they butcher the spelling), his father says only this: "My son is 24 years old and he knows his own mind." Full stop. No enthusiasm there, but I see that he's still shocked that his first-born is about to marry someone of another race, so strange-looking, so foreign.

Josh insists on the smallest possible wedding, and his parents—with no conviction about the event—are happy to oblige. We're married in September 1940 in the backyard of a house belonging to the widow of an American missionary to China. In Cambridge, Massachusetts. I wear a full-length slim Chinese dress of fine cream-colored silk, patterned with peonies (not white, which is the color of death). The dress, a *qipao,* is form-fitting and has a high collar, the same kind of dress that I wore to parties in Peking, only longer and with more modest side slits. It's what all fashionable Chinese women wear. I carry a flowing red bouquet, red the color of good fortune, in China. Josh wears a pinstriped suit. At the wedding are Josh's parents, his sister and his two brothers, including the one who's a Communist. Also Josh's best friend Willy and his wife, and one of my friends from Yenching (also in Chinese dress), and the Episcopalian minister. Of course, no one from my family is there, certainly not my mother. And my father's dead. Willy's the one who gives the bride away, and I say why not, because this is a silly tradition anyway, as though a bride can't think for herself.

Here's a photo of us standing on the porch after the wedding, Josh now with an overcoat on, and I in a mid-calf *qipao* with deeper slits and shoes with fashionable bows. We're looking ready to burst with expectation of happiness and with permission now to plunge deep into our relationship.

———

IN THE BACKGROUND, HOWEVER, THERE'S THAT VERY BIG problem of the Chinese Exclusion Act. Here's the thing: even though Josh and I are married, I cannot become an American citizen. America doesn't want me, because I'm Chinese. Why exclude only the Chinese? Because years ago, voters in California thought there were already too many Chinese in

America, back when lawmakers and newspapers and some labor union leaders thought the Chinese were a terrible "Yellow Peril" and that no more Chinese should ever again settle in America. America no longer needed "coolies" to hammer out their railroads or dig their gold mines or plant their vineyards and harvest their grapes. American workers thought Chinese workers would take their jobs, even though Americans themselves would never have worked for the pittance (and sometimes no wages at all) paid to the Chinese. Congress passed the Chinese Exclusion Act in 1882, slamming the door on the Chinese, and only the Chinese.

Does this mean that I'm stuck forever in limbo, that I can never become an American, even though I'm married to an American? It seems so. I'm insulted to be considered a Yellow Peril, even though we have similarly insulting terms for these white people (foreign devil, big-nose people). But I can deal with insults. I'm strong and I choose my battles. I can be completely charming even when I'm insulted. I save my moves for the Long Game. I don't fire off at the short-term stuff. To others I must not show weakness, ever. I do not flinch. I do not give up.

We damn the torpedoes and go full steam ahead. Without the slightest honeymoon, we move straight to Chicago and to Josh's university where we live in his basement apartment on the South Side, with little light and lots of cockroaches. I make it my business to get rid of the roaches: *done.* We live a typical graduate student life—little money, little time for anything but study. I work as a research assistant and learn to cook, and we invite friends over for cheap but exuberant dinners, cooked by me. We go to 25-cent movie matinees.

We talk incessantly about politics—Chinese politics and American politics. We agonize about the Nazis in Europe as well as the Japanese in Asia. Josh even goes to a Communist cell meeting, and he returns to say he found it full of hot air and jockeying for position among competing factions. But he toys with going back for another meeting. We discuss the lack of strong political leadership in China, and we worry about the possibility that the Soviet Communists might dominate the Chinese Communists. I say that *no* one can dominate our country. They can try, they can invade and beat us up, but they'll never win. The Russians can't tell us what to do. The Japanese can't either. They can't win! But we know Japan is driving deeper and deeper into southeast Asia and the Pacific islands. Japan is getting cozy with Nazi Germany.

There is one thing we never discuss, even with our friends, and that's my visa status. My student visa has lapsed, and now I'm illegal. An illegal alien. No official is paying any attention, no one has contacted me, no one has come looking for me. We live a simple student life and keep our mouths shut. I've become very good at keeping my mouth shut about what's really going on.

Then on December 7, 1941 Japanese warplanes attack the American Navy at Pearl Harbor. For the U.S., it's absolutely the end of the world as they knew it. Nearly 2,500 sailors and others are killed, war ships are sunk in harbor and fighter planes destroyed as they sit haplessly on the ground. America has been caught completely flat-footed. This Day of Infamy, as it comes to be called, is unimaginable to Americans and they are shocked beyond all measure. I am not shocked, having known Japanese attacks and Japanese bombing, but like all my American friends I never thought it could happen here in America, my place of refuge.

Suddenly America is at war, charging full-bore into World War II. At last! America will have to fight after all, on China's side against Japan in all of Asia and in the Pacific. American troops are called up, Army and Navy; fifty million men are drafted. It took Pearl Harbor to wake up America. They'll have to help China, now. They need China as a buttress against Japan. At the dawn of 1942, from the dim window-well of our basement apartment, I look out and I write:

"This year, I feel certain, we will see up there a horse, red-bronze, mane streaming to tail, nostrils flaming with sparks shot up from mighty hooves as he, the Firehorse, gallops down to greet us here on earth."

To the rescue! It's the Year of the Horse, and China will survive. I'm sure of it. The U.S. War Department now needs to recruit men who can speak Chinese or Japanese, which are two languages few Americans know how to speak. Josh is offered the chance to work in the War Department in Washington, the "Pentagon", instead of being sent to one of the battle fronts. Even *I* am offered the chance to help the war effort by working at the Pentagon. Here's my chance to help fight against Japan. But do they know I'm illegal? Do they care? Would all parties silently agree not to mention visa status, in the interest of fighting Japan?

Of course we would. We do exactly that. We stay silent. I begin to work long, long hours at the Pentagon to support the American attempt to Save China. To save China was my original cause, back when I was a student in Peking, so I tackle this task with everything I've got. Around this time, the lawmakers in Washington begin to realize that you cannot have China as your ally in fighting Japan, while at the same time refusing to grant citizenship to Chinese. It doesn't make common sense. So, after deliberations and posturing in Washington, in 1943 Congress finally repeals the Chinese Exclusion Act, over 60 years after it first took effect. It's the attack on Pearl Harbor that makes American Congressmen and diplomats and businessmen see the Chinese as GOOD and the Japanese as BAD, in the way they have of classifying foreigners as either Good or Bad.

Now the American public is practically hysterical about the "Japs." The U.S. Army issues a booklet titled *How to Spot a Jap*, full of lurid comparisons between the Noble Chinese and the suddenly Lowly Japanese. Americans are supposed to figure out how to tell the difference between a so-called Jap and a so-called Chinaman. It's a terrible time to be an Asian walking on a street in America. Along the coastlines, lights are turned off and blackout curtains pulled tight to hide American houses from Japanese or German aircraft or submarines. It's a dark time, literally, in American history, when the very survival of America seems to be at stake.

In all this dark, I decide to keep on hiding my illegal status, for fear of being deported into the Chinese war zone. I've been illegal for three years now, and I'm terribly afraid that even though I can now legally apply for citizenship, the immigration authorities won't give me amnesty after the fact. I feel frozen, in limbo: I'm not an American and I'm not likely ever to be treated like a true American (just look at the way they're putting Japanese-American *citizens* into camps. Does American citizenship mean nothing, if you're Asian?)

But maybe I'm not Chinese either—to those in China. Just look at my closest family, my mother and Huiyin, and you see how I'm rejected for having married a white American. Plus, the Japanese army would consider me a westerner. In Peking, since their Pearl Harbor attack, they're now rounding up westerners and sending them off to POW camps, forcing them into hard labor under the glare of armed Japanese guards. No more making nice with Western powers; to Japan all westerners are enemies now, excepting only the Germans and Italians, the Axis powers.

I'm not American, and to my family I'm not Chinese. I have no country, and the whole world is at war.

Just to be safe, Josh and I agree not to have any kids until this world war is over. If we were to have a child, that child would be "Eurasian", "Interracial" (that word!). And if something were to happen to Josh, as the mother of a half-Chinese half-white child, I'd be an outcast in both China and America, and so would my child. I think: no one in America or in China would ever marry a widow with a Eurasian kid. In China, half-Chinese children are often bullied by their schoolmates for having brown hair and big noses. In America it would be the same, but reversed: bullied for looking Chinese.

Meanwhile, without even knowing it, we're breaking another law. Virginia law forbids interracial cohabitation and interracial marriages. Such relationships are called "miscegenation" (one of the few words I'm forced to look up when I first hear it). Virginia is where Josh and I live and work. At the Pentagon we both work long hours to help the war effort against Japan, often coming home after dark and going out before dawn. We don't have the time to make new friends in the apartment building—and the other building residents are equally busy, everyone thinking only about this terrible war we've all been swept into. I know I'm seen as a curiosity but evidently nothing more than that. In any case, whether they didn't notice or didn't care, no Virginia authority comes knocking. Had they knocked, we would have been astonished to learn about this miscegenation law. (The law is not repealed until the famous *Loving v. Virginia* case in 1967).

We wonder whether the war will ever end. War has been raging for as long as we've known each other; we've never known peace together. We lie low and stay in our tiny apartment, we work hard at the War Department, and we just stay mum about my visa status. We tell no one I'm illegal. Doubly illegal if you consider the miscegenation laws.

––––––––––––

THEN SUDDENLY I DISCOVER I'M PREGNANT. WE PANIC. If I'm illegal, discovered, and deported, then Josh will be separated from his child. I'd have to return to war-torn China with a half-white baby in tow, facing rejection by my own family and overall rejection by the Chinese. I fear being a pariah on both shores.

We're now forced to tell Josh's parents about my pregnancy and my illegal status. His father Hits The Roof and his mother breaks down in tears, because they see that we're at the point of no return. After heated discussion it's decided that I must seek legal status, right away, never mind the risk of deportation, because otherwise our young family will be forced to live in the shadows indefinitely. I must bite the bullet and risk losing my American shelter from war, in order to gain American citizenship. It's worth the chance, Josh and I decide. And we must move fast on this, because I'm already three months pregnant and it will soon show badly.

So I go to the Chinese Embassy here in Washington, D.C. and apply for a Chinese passport. The Embassy chooses to overlook that I'm applying for this passport after I've already lived in the U.S. for over 5 years. Perhaps winking (again I can't be sure, but I play it straight), they issue me a passport. Then with this Chinese passport Josh and I drive all the way to Montreal, in Canada. We actually leave the U.S. in order to apply for a visa for me to *enter* the

U.S. again. Because Congress lifted their Chinese ban two years ago, the U.S. immigration officials in Montreal can now grant me a general visa (not just a student visa). And with this visa I enter the U.S.—legally. We drive back to Washington like crazy happy teenagers on a mad escapade, laughing, singing, windows rolled down so that the wind rushes through the speeding car.

But back in Washington, I cannot rest yet. Although I'm now legal, this visa will expire, and unless I gain citizenship I'll lapse back into illegality. Josh's folks are relentlessly nagging me about this. So, I apply to become one of the 105 Chinese to be granted citizenship each year, under the terms of the new immigration rules for Chinese. It takes time to go through this process, and I fail to complete it before our daughter is born. In immigration-speak, she's born to a Chinese Alien, but at least this Alien is legal.

Our daughter! Born in 1945, right after the U.S. drops two horrific atom bombs on Japan, killing 150,000 people in an instant. An instant. Japan surrenders, as Germany and Italy had surrendered earlier this year. World War II is finally over, leaving at least 50 million people dead. Josh and I decide to name our daughter *An,* a Chinese word for Peace. Bureaucracy being what it is, An soon becomes Ann.

But *Bian An* is her name. Proudly I take her to the office, strapped to my chest with a large cloth *baofu,* Chinese-style. My colleagues celebrate her arrival as though she were a just-discovered exotic creature, finding humor that Peace, *An,* has been born into the War Department.

Conveniently, Josh's mother's given name was Annie. She and Josh's father are much relieved when our baby proves not to look Too Chinese. At birth she has lots of soft black hair that stands straight up, as though she's gotten quite a fright. But after six months she loses that black hair and her new hair grows back blonde. Amazingly, she looks just like any other little blonde American kid. Josh's parents relax: *look at this cute little kid!* Welcome, daughter-in-law Nancy Zhou!

I don't mention to my in-laws how I wish our baby were a boy, not a girl. Boys are prized in China; girls are not. If I ever have to return to my family in China, they will be much less interested in me because I have only a girl. And that girl doesn't even look Chinese.

My mother-in-law drags little An to the most expensive photography studio in Boston, to have An's picture taken. I am not in the picture. The photo is framed and shown around to the rest of the extended Bennett family, to say: See, not such an oddity after all. Josh and Nancy's baby looks just like any other American baby. No uptilted eyes. No black hair or dark skin like me. In fact she's got freckles!

As An becomes a wide-eyed toddler with vaguely curly blonde hair, I'm annoyed to find that strangers who see me with my own child assume I must be the babysitter. Hired help. And when Josh is with us, they think that An must be Josh's daughter from a previous marriage to a white woman. Obviously the three of us don't quite look like a family. People stare at us to try to figure out who's who.

And by the way, I still wear my slim and slit-side Chinese dresses, everywhere. My long hair is done up in a bun, with a Chinese hair ornament plunged into it. Sometimes I carry a Chinese silk handbag. You see, with my dark skin I don't want people to think that I'm a black woman, because it's dangerous to be black in America. I'm shocked that black people are treated so badly, even attacked, not only in the South, but here in Washington, and in Chicago, and sometimes even in

Boston. A terrible, terrible thing I've learned about America is that it's never been safe for black people anywhere in this land. To be safe I'd much rather have people think I'm a foreigner wearing my weird national get-up. Less dangerous that way, though it's irritating when they come up to me and speak pidgin English ("You wantee help findee street?"). They mean well. When you're here for the long haul, it's better to be underestimated than overestimated.

Nanjing, 1946

CHAPTER 6

When Does It End?
Yet Another War

With the end of World War II, Josh wonders whether to go back to Chicago to finish his PhD degree. He's received a prestigious fellowship to do this, but he's impatient to return to China as soon as possible. And I cannot wait to go back to China. How I've missed Peking! In my mind I'm always painting pictures, pictures of its streets, its smells, its noises—the street clatter and the quavering, haunting music, but mostly just the sound of Mandarin spoken all around me, Chinese faces instead of a sea of white. Most of all I want to see my family again, my family whom I've missed beyond all imagining, my brothers and even my mother. I say to Josh, please let's go to China. Please.

No one knows what will happen at Yenching University now that the war is over, and Josh can't teach there anyway without a PhD. I urge him to find us another way back to Peking. So he decides to try to go back to China as a diplomat. I'm enthusiastic about this! After all, my father was a diplomat, and his job allowed us to travel the world and to live in grand houses with servants to cook and clean. So, Josh enters the United States Information Service (USIS).

Because he speaks fluent Chinese, they send him to China and we're both delighted. The U.S. Embassy there is in Nanjing (Nanking), not Peking. But no matter, it's China, and Josh and I expect to be able to travel all over China, now that the Japanese soldiers have been driven out.

Because I haven't yet gotten my U.S. citizenship, I don't want to go back to China until it's crystal-clear that I'm an American. I haven't forgotten what China is like under war conditions. I'm afraid that American authorities could prevent me from returning to America with my husband and baby. So I stay behind in Boston, with our baby, until—finally—I'm granted full-fledged U.S. citizenship. At last! Josh had left for Nanjing months ago, but I earn a bear hug from Josh's father, while his mother scoops up little An and rocks her giddy.

American passport in hand, I pack up baby An and we take the train from Boston to San Francisco, just the two of us. Then we board a steamship bound for Shanghai. An is not a year old; on the ship she tries out her new baby steps, only to tumble down hard on the deck of the swaying boat. (Being cautious, she doesn't try walking again until months later and on solid ground in Nanjing). In Shanghai, Josh meets us at the boat, and the three of us travel by train to Nanjing. We live in a German-style house next door to a large but empty estate. Nearly all the other Embassy families live in accommodations grouped together in a compound around the American Embassy. But I want to live in China, not in an outpost of America; so we find that separate house to rent for ourselves.

Then, for me, a terrible discovery: Nanjing is very unstable, despite the fact that the Japanese have departed. Supposedly the city is now governed by the Republic of China, the Nationalists. But conditions here are very bad. Much of the physical damage from the Japanese air and ground attacks remains evident. The population has been decimated and terrorized by the Japanese massacres that occurred not long ago. And inflation is out of control. Inflation is catastrophic. From our kitchen window I can see people running down the street with paper money in sacks and even rackety wheelbarrows, desperate to buy goods before prices go up, as they go up every day, sometimes every hour. People cannot buy enough food to feed themselves. On the streets they beg for food. They do not trust the money. They do not trust the government. The political situation is very hard to read. Everyone is very nervous.

There are riots, occasionally in Nanjing, but more often in other cities. These are "rice riots" that flare up when people line up at stores for rice that runs out, and then fight with police over the nothing that remains. There is not enough food. There is terrible disease everywhere, visible everywhere you look—gummy eyes, open sores, wracking coughs. You can stay home. You can try to look the other way. But there is no denying the desperation.

The Government makes pronouncements offering high-minded goals that are meant to inspire the citizenry, but all the citizens want is a bowl of rice and freedom from violence. They are tired, beaten down by war and all its dislocations, suffering seemingly endless deprivation, endless loss, close to exhaustion of their remarkable stoicism. Writing these words in a comfortable house, I know how lucky I am, but in my mind there is a growing sense of the ominous, this thing that sneaks up on you and then rips out your heart.

It seems as though Mao Zedong's Red Army, now called the People's Liberation Army, the PLA, are fighting their way toward Nanjing, bringing with them a new way of work, a new way of life, a shared spirit of optimism and a theory of how to deal with the ravages of war. It's a spirit notably lacking in the Nationalist government, where corruption is rife, the government police disheartened, the military often undisciplined and in disarray. We're told the PLA arrive in successive cities wearing cloth shoes and bound leggings tattered by long journey, and they may carry hoes instead of rifles, but they walk tall, maybe even with swagger. This is an army of liberation, liberation from the Japanese, yes, but now also liberation from the "imperialists" such as the Americans and other westerners. This is nothing less than a revolution, not just a civil war.

But we Americans seem bound to stand with the Nationalist government. I'm at war with myself about this. I'm married to an American, and I've become an American citizen. But I'm Chinese, I have deep loyalty to China, and I can't help admiring this army of peasants, the PLA, for fighting the Japanese even without the guns that America supplies to the Nationalists, and for showing Japan and the West what Chinese victory looks like, what Chinese discipline looks like. Inside myself I often cheer, but outside I must always stand with the Americans, and the Americans—for reasons I can't fathom—have decided to side with the Nationalists in this civil war.

Finally, I hear from my mother, by letter. One of my cousins has joined the People's Liberation Army; she marches with the New Fourth Army. An aunt is also in the PLA. My cousin Sukie, who'd been beaten and arrested by the Japanese over ten years ago, finally left China in 1941 and married a Chinese-American in California (I knew that). Huiyin and Sicheng have returned to Peking from the hinterlands, but I don't care, I won't see Huiyin, after her betrayal. Even my *mother* has accepted Josh, so she and Huiyin are at odds again, as before. Meanwhile my mother has turned down an offer to serve on one of the Nationalist Government councils. My family is riven by this war, I now see.

How I wish the Nationalists and the Communists could come together and forge a coalition government! That's the hope of many in the American Embassy here, especially those with long experience in China, and they work hard to negotiate this. But despite various hopeful signs, the Nationalists and the Communists do not come together; instead their clashes grow more serious. Meanwhile, in America there are businesses and churchmen and the "China Lobby" of politicians and press that will not tolerate anything but a China ruled by Nationalists.

How I dread this terrible burgeoning estrangement, this conflict between my husband's country and my family's country! I'm terrified about this fighting that creeps toward us without relent, black clouds belching out to the horizon, bringing fear of death from the skies, and separation by endless cruel war.

Josh is working at the American Embassy, and I start teaching English at Nanjing University. At home we have a cook and a babysitter, so An is looked after while we're both at work. In February 1948, about 18 months into our time in Nanjing, I have a baby daughter, born around the time that it seemed as though the Nationalists might prevail in the civil war. We name our new daughter *Jing*, for "quiet", maybe so that we can tell people that our daughters are named Peace and Quiet, always good for a laugh. But in truth Jing is a lovely Chinese name, which readily becomes "Jean". *An Jing*, Ann and Jean, we now call them. And Jing is a beauty, stunning black eyes with skin as dark as An's is light. A real

Chinese baby, and what a baby! We're happy beyond measure, even though again I wish it were a boy, for reasons of Chinese preference. But a baby is a baby whether boy or girl, and to my giddy delight this baby looks Chinese. She is cherished.

An, always cautious, after an initial inspection claims that Jing is "her" baby. Right away she starts looking after her, watching anxiously as Jing later begins to crawl around and explore, running to tell me if Jing is going too close to something, or too far from something, or any small thing that might threaten Jing. Thus we give An her nickname, *Guai-guai*, which translates roughly as "Goody-goody." Jing we call *Mei-mei*, which means "little sister" but has also a beautiful sound, like a soft sigh in the evening.

With conditions safe for travel (only temporarily, it would turn out), Josh and I drive often into the countryside around Nanjing, and he's enthralled once again by China's temples, Buddhas, and stone statues, many from the Ming Dynasty. The statues can be scattered, solitaire, or random, but they're always majestic—a stone warrior standing alone before towering hills, a flaring stone lion serving as one side of an otherwise thatched peasant dwelling. Josh pulls over to take pictures, and sometimes he puts An atop a stone lion's back. Then there's little An in a kerchief, staring up at the tusks of an enormous stone elephant near the Ming tombs of Nanjing, or standing beside a temple monster at some other random stop on our forays from the city.

We climb the large and hulking Nanjing city wall, often with friends, and in happy conversation we walk for miles along the crumbling fortification. One time we take An up the wall, and from that day I've kept a picture that Josh took of An seated next to me on the wall, toward Purple Mountain, looking over seemingly all of China, farmland and paddies stretching beyond vision and beyond camera. China, so beautiful to both Josh and me.

I TAKE THE TRAIN TO PEKING TO VISIT MY FAMILY, WHO have moved closer to the Forbidden City, to *Xiang Bizi* (Elephant Nose Hutong, because the hutong curves back on itself). I bring both An and Jing to show them to my mother and brothers. My mother, whom I haven't seen in nine years, greets me with unusual emotion, sobbing with her chin down and her eyes watering with happiness and a shaking of shoulders that she tries hard to hide. She's overwhelmed by these two little grandchildren she's never seen before. An she considers a curious sight, looking so like a *waiguoren* (foreigner) that she cannot believe she's a Zhou, a Liang. But Jing she finds enchanting, with her round Chinese face and dark eyes and ready laughter. Jing is a wonder! She's already telling stories (just like me) even though she hasn't any words yet. She points and declares and nods and tilts her head sideways to make a point. My mother smiles at her, from ear to ear, my mother who hardly ever smiled at me, when I was growing up. I sense she's forgiven me for leaving Peking with a *waiguoren,* for leaving my family during the Japanese invasion. Now she can only exult quietly at her new-found granddaughters.

Does she even remember her harshness toward Josh, when he and I decided to marry? The way she and my father humiliated us? Has she put aside her seeming hatred of me, her lacerating disapproval of my choices? Has she forgiven me for defying my father and thus (to her) inviting his death? We're Chinese: she doesn't say and I don't ask. It's a game of willful ignorance of our personal history.

But it's not a game. In my memory she was an aggressive Mahjong player; she played "like a demon," a friend once told me. Through the courtyards you'd hear the tap-tapping of Mahjong tiles, occasional laughter, occasional cries, cigarette smoke hovering overhead, her friends leaning into the game or gesturing for the servants to bring more tea or wine. At those times, she'd pay no attention to us children. She was Sishun, Liang Qichao's eldest, and don't you ever forget that, her demeanor would say. Off to the side would be Po, Liang Qichao's second wife, nearly always deferential to my mother, as she still is, even now. I think: my mother will always hang onto her pride. She'll always be Liang Sishun.

Yet now her eyes have grown softer. She no longer stares at me. If the Mahjong tiles are around, I don't see them. For once she wants just to be with us. Po, who was always the one who nurtured me, has been pushed aside during my visit. Sishun rules this household. She allows Po only minutes with me, here and there. And thus I see how my mother Sishun loves me. It's a nettled love, and it's tightly wound, but it's unmistakable now.

This is a time I'll never forget. The graceful family courtyard, the moon gate, the willow trees bending over the group of us, my mother and brothers and me, sitting in rattan chairs sipping green tea from the familiar teacups and talking, talking, talking to cover the nine lost years, years lost to war and separation. I am home in Peking again, and how I have missed my family. One of my brothers also has children, and we watch our toddler children stagger around and occasionally engage with one another. An speaks only Chinese, and she's completely at home. Jing, still a baby, isn't old enough to speak beyond "Mama." I'm swept up in lightness and stories and laughter, and at night I lie down in consummate joy at my return to Peking.

But the visit lasts only a few weeks. When I look back on it years from now I'll see it was a cruel tease, hopes lifted and then slammed down and shattered into pieces. I should have known even then.

Beyond the moon gate, at the outer gate, I bid my mother goodbye, arms around her only lightly because she's not a hugger, and we're both superstitious enough to know that if you hug someone goodbye it's like saying you don't think you'll see them again. Like saying you expect them to die. Inauspicious. In China long life is treasured, the highest hope, but it's never taken for granted. Survival is never taken for granted.

My mother casts a last fond gaze at the granddaughters she's barely met. We're to go to the train station by pedi-cab, pedaled by a panting youth who will struggle with the weight of our luggage. As the pedaling starts, I look back at my mother and I wave as she turns to re-enter the gate. She doesn't see me wave. It's the last time I'll ever see my mother, but I don't know it at the time. This memory scorches me every time I return to it, and I can't help returning to it.

CHAPTER 7

The Price of War

B ack in Nanjing, I find that the tide has turned dramatically against the Nationalist forces. In mid-November, all of the roughly 800 American military advisors and their dependents are ordered by Washington to return immediately to the U.S. By the evening of their departure, the belongings they leave behind are looted. Washington advises the departure of the wives and children of American civilians, including Embassy staff. The destination is a camp for displaced persons (a "DP camp") in Manila. Josh is very worried about our safety—we're living away from the American Embassy compound, and the looting has jarred him, along with other dangerous incidents that mark the suddenly obvious unraveling of social fabric. Whatever community, whatever center position between the warring parties had held till now, is evaporating.

Josh wants us to go to a safe place. He assures me that this will be only temporary, and so I take An and baby Jing with me and fly to Manila, along with the wives and children of other Embassy staff. In my passport photograph, I have both my girls on my lap, An looking dumbfounded, Jing hollering with wide-open mouth. I make sure we're all in the same photograph, so that no authorities will separate my children from me as we cross borders. And now I must call my girls Ann and Jean, the names on the passport. No more An and Jing. We must seem like the Americans we are.

Conditions in Manila are uncomfortable, but with all the fighting throughout Asia, I remind myself that I have nothing to complain about. Nothing. True, we live in a grimy thatched hut in the camp, Ann dropping her few baby toys through holes in the planked floor, and everyone shaking out shoes each morning to dislodge any scorpions that might have scuttled there overnight. The weather is oppressively hot. When I go to the market to buy vegetables I'm robbed at knifepoint, and this by *day*, not night. At night we hear gunfire. "Rats", they explain, but we know better.

The camp is rife with rumor. Every day I go to a depot at the camp to listen to Army radio, trying to find out what's going on in China. What I hear convinces me that I cannot stay in Manila. If I am here, and Josh is there in Nanjing, and the Communists come to power, then I probably couldn't go back to China while there's fighting and negotiation. That would mean the girls and I might be separated from Josh for a long time. But if the girls and I are there in China together with Josh and some other American officials, there's a chance that we can all stay as the American diplomats seek to work out an accommodation with the new government. Maybe the U.S. will recognize the new government. Then maybe China will allow us to stay. These are my thoughts—call them desperate if you want.

I insist on returning to China. Josh agrees, with some hesitation. Fearing that the window's closing, I take matters into my own hands and with what's left of my month's allowance I buy plane tickets back to Shanghai. Flights into China are ridiculously cheap, because most foreigners are trying to fly out, not in. In Shanghai, people are fighting to crowd onto the planes out of China. Meanwhile planes into Shanghai have few passengers, because few want to enter a war zone. Thus in one of those half-empty planes I return to China with my kids, landing in Shanghai, along with some other wives and children with husbands in Nanjing.

Now there's a frantic exchange of telegrams between the Ambassador in Nanjing and the State Department in Washington, with the Consulate in Shanghai chiming in and with Washington clearly annoyed by my insistence on being in China. I'll always be Chinese, and I'm stubborn besides. Finally, the Americans relent and allow us to fly on, to Nanjing. At the airfield, with little Ann clutching my hand, and baby Jean strapped to my chest in a Chinese *baofu,* I rush down the steps onto the tarmac, into Josh's arms. Home!

I settle back into our house. Though the wartime situation in Nanjing continues to deteriorate, and chaos threatens each day, I only want to be in China, as long as there's hope for us to live here. Whatever the outcome of this cruel war, I want to live that hope, my dearest hope: that the Communists and Nationalists can come together in a coalition government, ending the killing.

Yet that hope diminishes. Nanjing is spiraling downward. Neither side in this war will yield. For the Communists, this is a war of liberation. For the Nationalists, and increasingly for the Americans, it is a war against Soviet domination because many Americans, not knowing Chinese history, think that the Soviet Union is going to control the Chinese Communists. In the middle, the people suffer, fleeing from one place to another. One Embassy observer writes about Nanjing:

> "The hardest sight is the refugees. No matter who they
> are, or where or when, all refugees look alike—cold,
> hungry, unshaven, forlorn, and lost. They don't know

where they came from or where they are going. They are just wherever they are and don't know what to do about it. This is not only true of the Chinese; it is almost as true of the foreigners, who have a pretty good idea they will get out of the country, although they know some of them may not. Even the missionaries who have been in China for decades are just as helpless, and who can blame them. They have only our word that they should move on—somewhere, anywhere, but move, and so they move. When I think how many lives are being uprooted today and all the days around it and all that it means....
And still they pour through by the thousands, on and on."

When the People's Liberation Army finally marches into Nanjing unopposed in April 1949, the Nationalist government simply walks away without a fight, and there's an uneasy peace if you can call it that. In some parts of the city, some people start looting, but the looting is limited. The Communists take charge. They do not steal food, nor do they bully (as the Nationalist troops were often known to do). They need to figure out how to run the city, keep the lights on and the water running. They need to keep the economy from crashing altogether. They're only partly successful, but their earnestness is hard to miss. I'm filled with hope that this Communist victory, the taking over of Nanjing, will finally bring peace and accommodation.

On the evening of April 24th, I write to Josh's family to describe these past two days. The top of my letter proclaims "Liberation Day," underlined twice. I can't hide my excitement:

[April 23] *"Early in the morning we heard that all police had evacuated during the night; the Mayor's*

house (a couple of blocks from us) was being looted;
the President's house was being looted; shops, especially
rice and flour shops, were being looted; and mean-
while thousands of Nationalist troops were retreating
in tight formation up the street right past USIS. I
was at home facing such crises as water stoppage and
no market for US dollars. By noon however, matters
appeared much more settled. We had managed to fill
all the bathtubs and extra storage tanks before the
water stopped altogether. The last Nationalist soldier
had marched up the street to his doom. Nanking was
empty—and quiet.

After lunch, we were reminded that this was the
day we had been waiting for, and therefore not a day
to be spent at home. Having made arrangements for
the children to be cared for in case something hap-
pened to us, we sallied out. First we went downtown.
The streets were full of people standing around laugh-
ing and joking, waiting for something to happen....

[April 24] *"When we turned on the radio at break-*
fast at eight, the station was Communist, announcing
that they had taken over the city at seven. Right after
breakfast we dashed down to USIS in a car, just in
time to see the People's Liberation Army marching
down the same street the retreating Nationalists had
marched up so soon before. Thousands of people were
out to watch. We had a wonderful time taking pictures,
picking up leaflets, watching the soldiers sing. Later
we went out on bikes for greater freedom of action."

We've just witnessed a revolution. A Revolution. But
some say we've been "occupied"—as though the PLA were

some alien force! Because it's my life, my only chance to live in China, I carry hope in my heart, hope that the triumphant Communists will allow us to stay in China, allow for a chance for reconciliation.

Yet the American Embassy is at odds with itself, some favoring an effort to work with leaders of this revolution, against others insisting that Chinese Communists are Communists first and Chinese second—that is, loyal to the Soviet Union. The Soviet Union has become such a source of anxiety that *the Americans are even helping to rebuild Japan* to resist Soviet Communism. No kidding. I'm speechless at this complete turnabout. All of this is not for my ears. Josh does not speak of it. But I can see his enormous internal conflict, his desire to stay in China and to help rebuild, not to prolong warfare. And he knows better than anyone that my future life is in the hands of something very big and very unpredictable: the relations between the United States and China.

But Josh is a small voice in a very noisy American presence in China, and there's an even noisier argument raging in Washington. What can he do, when the most experienced voices on China are disregarded and even targeted by politicians in Washington seeking their own reelection, however false their issues? When the People's Liberation Army establishes one of its headquarters right next door to our house, Josh says we must be especially careful not to provoke the Communist soldiers. The soldiers next door are individually pleasant, terribly young, and slightly bewildered at their sudden responsibilities in Nanjing. One guard at their gate scolds 4-year old Ann for riding her tricycle in front of him on the sidewalk, back and forth, back and forth, back and forth, very annoying, but her response to his snappish words is to inform him primly, in perfect Chinese (this little blonde girl), that he should know that she's not allowed to ride in the street. She must stay on the sidewalk. The soldier smiles despite himself.

Another time, less funny, some of the soldiers steal the duck swimming in the wooden tub in our backyard, presumably because they're desperate for something to eat. When Ann discovers that the duck is gone, there's no way not to tell her that her duck's been eaten (we hadn't told her that it was headed for the cooking pot anyway). Ann's wails of sheer shock can't have gone unnoticed by the soldiers next door. I explain to her: people have to eat.

These are small events. The ugly bigger picture is that Nanjing is falling apart, ever faster, with runaway inflation partly caused by desperate currency maneuvers and daily life driven by an exploding black market. I write to a friend in the U.S.:

"As an assistant professor at a university, my salary this month was 14 million yuan ($14 US) in cash, plus a bonus of 8 rolls of U.S. toilet paper, 2 gallons of kerosene, 30 pounds of rice, a bundle of sticks for fuel, and an empty half-gallon glass bottle without any cork. This is what professors are supposed to live on with eggs at 10 thousand yuan and a banana at 30 thousand."

The scarcity of food spreads wide. Beggars in the streets become more numerous and far more aggressive, and who can blame them? Disease lurks everywhere, in the water, in the lack of sanitation, in the debris and rodents in the streets. The Nationalists, having left the city, are trying to choke off the Communists. They've blockaded Shanghai. The U.S. had given planes to the Nationalists to fight the Japanese, and now the Nationalists use these planes to fly over Nanjing, trying to bomb the utilities and transportation hubs, to cripple the Communist effort to run the city. To avoid groundfire, the planes fly high and often miss their mark, killing civilians.

I teach my little girls to run and hide under the sofa or table or bed when they hear the air raid sirens start to wail. The sirens start as a growl and rise to a shriek, and the terror is real. I cry out, *feiji! feiji!* (airplanes! airplanes!) and we all run for cover. This is no way to live.

Even so, I try to live a normal life. I try to pretend that this is all a temporary aberration, that eventually all parties will sit down and form a coalition government to include both sides in this war, and that the air attacks will stop. We can't afford to have me quit my job at Nanjing University, and because our babysitter isn't able to deal with both Ann and Jean, I enroll Ann in a public preschool about three miles away through crowded streets. Ann is the only *waiguoren* in this school, but she speaks perfect Chinese—in fact she doesn't speak a word of English. So she's Chinese, even though she's still blonde. It's a rough and ready school, a dirt schoolyard, some rudimentary equipment, and supervision by young Chinese preschool teachers who keep order but give no instruction. Ann adjusts quickly.

But now whenever the air raid sirens start their terrifying wail, I grab baby Jean and take a pedicab to the school to gather up Ann. We hurry back home together, the pedicab pumped by a man as frightened as we are. I have no idea whether and where the bombs might fall. I grow deeply afraid. I'm afraid for my two small children, and I ask myself how we can survive in a Nanjing that's become a dangerous war zone. Eventually I decide no more preschool for Ann, I quit my job despite the financial impact, and I stay home now with my two little girls, crouching down when we hear the warning sirens too loud, listening to the explosions as the bombs fall. They fall in the distance, so far. And in winter the raids are less frequent, because of winter's cloud cover: rain and fog.

But now it's late spring, no more cloud cover, and my worry rises to near-panic. I find myself turning to writing as my little girls are napping. Writing has always been my source of comfort, my vent for despair and sheer fright. I imagine a woman-god, *Guanyin*, who will show compassion and protect my small children from war, but the cadence of my poem suggests Christian prayer, the King James Bible. I ask for help both from Chinese deities and from the western God:

"CHINESE PRAYER

Dear Goddess of Mercy,
Creator of beauty,
Thanks be to you for the clouds this dawn.
My woman-heart kneels,
My woman-heart feels
The ineffable peace of this dismal rain.
Ah, the dark clouds are comfort,
This drear chill sheer blessing,
We've been blessed with damp misery
Since the year's first month.
Dear Goddess of Mercy,
Kind giver of life, keep fettered your sunshine
Which only brings death.

Dear Goddess of Mercy,

Protectress of children,

My children have asked to go out in the sun.

They have gone to the river.

Why? Why should I shiver?

Childhood belongs to the warm white sun.

But the blue skies are clearing,

The west wind blows,

Gone is our safety with the year's fourth month.

Dear Goddess of Mercy,

Mother of women,

Our children forget there is death in clear skies.

Dear Goddess of Mercy

Who keeps us from peril,

Grant us this one day of deep spring peace.

Our home is vain shelter,

The streets are a welter

Of ditches and tunnels and cruel warning signs.

So if danger's without,

And no safety within,

Why strive to fetter

Perhaps life's last month?

Dear Goddess of Mercy,

Goddess all gentle,

Protect us from harm

If the dread siren blows.
Dear Goddess of Mercy,
Great Keeper of Souls!
What was that blast?
And this strange, black silence?
Dear Goddess of Mercy—"

(My poem ends with an imagined life-ending explosion.)

Sunshine Which Only Brings Death. The Dread Siren. This is how my mind works. This is how I try to control my terror that something crushing will happen to my little children. This is how I come to pray, pray as I was taught in church as a child. I want only that my daughters can live to grow up, to find a life away from war. I have no idea how to make this happen. I'm powerless but I'm a fighter. I never give up. We'll do what we have to do, to survive these endless wars.

In September 1949 Mao Zedong is about to proclaim the establishment of the People's Republic of China, and the PLA continues to drive the Nationalist leaders out of China, or what's left of the Nationalist leaders. There will be no coalition government between the Communists and the Nationalists. The westerners (including nearly all Americans) are forced to leave the country immediately. Josh tells me, *Go,* go now and I'll meet you after I help close our offices.

Knowing how many others will be converging on the train station, I hurriedly throw together some bags, grab Ann and Jean, hail a pedicab and head to the station to try to reach Shanghai, shouting *kuai-kuai kuai-kuai* (hurry, hurry) to the driver. The station is mobbed, westerners trying to push onto the trains, with luggage and pets and even golf bags (I think: crazy priorities, some of these westerners have). There's shouting and jostling and bureaucracy all at once, as officious agents examine our papers and decide who's to go and who's to wait for the next train. We wait for nearly 8 hours, until finally we're squeezed onto an already packed train. People without tickets sit on the roof of the train, clutching children and their meager belongings wrapped in cloth.

Reaching Shanghai, we're told to wait for over a week in a crowded, disheveled hotel that had once had pretensions to glamor. Now it's a site where westerners, once comfortably settled in China, are down to a suitcase and memories exchanged over the dwindling supply of booze. There are vain attempts at humor about having been kicked out of China. I don't drink, because it makes my face red. Besides, I don't need a drink to look upbeat; it's always easy for me to pretend.

Eventually we crowd onto a converted U.S. Army troop ship, the *S.S. General Gordon,* and I find myself in crew quarters with bunkbeds stacked up three or four levels (I can't even remember). Jean and I share a bunkbed at the bottom, and Ann is in the bunk just above us, and above her is a longtime friend, the wife of one of Josh's colleagues at the Embassy. We women are in our own bunkrooms, the men in other bunkrooms. The ship sets sail after some wrangling between the Nationalists (still clinging to the mainland) and the Communists. Less than an hour out of the dock, while we're still on the Whampoa (*Huangpu*) River sailing toward ocean, we're stopped by a Nationalist patrol ship wanting to search for contraband. After several hours of searching and the grilling of the ship's officers and crew, they let us go, and soon we reach the ocean, heading for Hong Kong.

With the ship all a-kilter (my imagination no doubt), there's no time to worry about anything beyond food and passage, passage to safety. We've been banished from China. I am dazed. For once I can't speak, I can't think, I can't feel. I never even had a chance to let my mother know that we're gone, gone from China. I wonder when and how she'll ever find out, amid these war conditions, mail now stalled, telephones non-existent, Peking in disarray like Nanjing and Shanghai. My mother won't know that I'm gone; she won't know for a long time.

In my heart there's a tearing sound, a ripping of my soul. I'd yearned for my family to be part of my life. I want my little girls to grow up seeing their grandmother and their uncles and aunts and cousins in Peking. But I'm being torn away from all I knew when young. I am as stone. I don't know yet that I'll never see my Peking again, I'll never see my mother again. The future is an aloneness that I never imagined, and it sneaks up on me stealthily over the years to come. Yet I go on with outward spirit, with determined and ceaseless optimism, for the sake of my children.

In a nightmare: the American continent is moving inexorably away from the Chinese continent, and I stretch to see my mother and my family across this divide. In this vision that never leaves me, I see them on the other side of the gap that yawns ever wider, like an earthquake opening up the ground between us, the jaws widening and widening, and my mother and brothers waving to me desperately as they recede, more and more distant from me. They become dots on a barren horizon. In my dream I call out wildly, crazed, to be reunited for even a moment, but I always wake up stunned. I know I must not cry. My crying stays inside me.

I am strong. I made a choice, maybe the wrong choice, but I will never say that to anyone or even to myself. I cannot think about this. I cannot discuss this.

Jiangsu Province, 1949

CHAPTER 8

The War Next Door

We land in Washington, probably because no one in the U.S. government knows what to do with us, stunned as they are by the Communist victory, by "the loss of China"—as though China was theirs to lose. Josh and I buy a small house in suburban Washington, and I try to live the life of the American Suburban Housewife, circa 1950. I shop at the supermarket, I make low-cost dinners, I learn to drive a car badly, I take care of two-year-old Jean, and I wait by the kitchen door each day for little Ann to walk home from kindergarten. Ann is being teased because she can't speak English, and she wears a too-big fuzzy brown coat that inspires the American kindergarteners to call her "the bear." Ann then has nightmares about a big bear, *xiong* (熊) she says —even the Chinese character looks like it has four feet and a big head, and Ann's frightened.

She's becoming very shy; she might have been born shy. But she's a diligent little girl, and determined (like me); and she does see humor quite easily, even in her plight. She's picking up English, and school soon becomes less baffling. Jean's a handful and a delight at home; she talks and tells us about everything she sees and everything she thinks. Josh and I are living the American Dream, I'm told, and I have to agree it isn't bad, not at all. The streets are clean, there's no starvation

or disease, and there are no war-wounded on the streets begging for rice. For once, very briefly, no war.

But in 1950 the Korean War breaks out. At first I'm
just glad we're not in Korea. But the Korean War drives
the American continent even farther from the Chinese
continent, and my Peking family on the other side of the
divide recedes still further. My nightmare takes stealthy
shape: shortly we're sent to Taiwan, where the Nationalists—having fled China—have taken up residence. It's clear
now that America has decided not to recognize the new
People's Republic of China, despite the opinions of many
of America's top experts and leaders. The reasons have to do
with American politics as much as Chinese politics. There
are disturbing threats coming from Washington, and anyone
who favors the People's Republic is accused of being a trai-
tor, or at least "soft on communism." I am chilled when I
hear this. I feel cornered. I have split vision: on one side the
China that I know, and on the other side the demonized
China flogged by politicians. The nightmare takes further
form, the divide yawns wider, slavering jaws of doom.

In Taiwan we live in Taipei, in a Japanese house dating
from Japan's earlier occupation of Taiwan, a house all of
wood and paper-clad sliding walls and floors of *tatami*, grass
matting. There's irony, if not satisfaction just in knowing
that Japan has now been driven out of this house it built.
Taipei has occasional earthquakes, causing the overhead
hanging lamps to pitch wildly back and forth, and pieces of
furniture to topple. Josh teases the girls by telling them the
earth might open up and swallow the whole house. The girls
sit wide-eyed, but they're game, always game for whatever
comes next. I'm raising them that way, because it's the only
way you can survive.

The U.S. Army has become a very big presence in Taiwan. Partly this is because of the Korean War, not far away. So now Ann goes to an American school that's been established by the U.S. Army for army children. She and Jean both master English and can speak it as fluently as Chinese. At home we have two "amahs", one Taiwanese and one Japanese. The girls scamper outside with both Chinese friends and American friends. They go back and forth between Chinese language and English, no difference. Josh scares them with Chinese and Japanese folk tales involving magic monkeys and dragons and monsters. A tutor comes once a week to teach the girls calligraphy. I go back to teaching, this time at the university in Taipei.

And now the full shock of the U.S. turnabout on Japan: *Japan,* so recently our enemy, is suddenly a friend to America, in the new-found fight against communism. I am stunned and dismayed. Has everyone suddenly forgotten what Japan did to China, the millions of Chinese they so deliberately killed? American military bases pop up in Japan and Taiwan, focused on China. Taipei sees military parades seemingly all the time, troops marching in front of a reviewing stand. The head of the Nationalist government, the durable, ever-pushy Chiang Kai-shek, watches high-stepping soldiers and tanks go by. Proto-fascism, some critics say.

I want to shout out the irony! But I do not.

War continues to dog us, thanks to the Korean War. The U.S. Army is everywhere, rain falling on brand-new but muddy roads they have yet to pave, everyone bumping around in Army jeeps, more Army families arriving every day. At school Ann learns the *Pledge of Allegiance,* the *Star-Spangled Banner,* and *She's a Grand Old Flag* ("She's the emblem of/ the land I love"—a land Ann's barely seen). In the schoolyard she and her classmates do calisthenics. To follow the drills, they're taught the difference between left and right. Josh finds this hilarious, joking that he's having trouble himself with the distinction, having started out on the left, and now fearing he's getting ensnared on the right.

I'd thought the end of World War II meant the end of war. Wrong! We're almost immediately swallowed again by war. In America, this Korean War is fanning the flames of anti-communism. Seemingly out of nowhere come Senators and others who outlandishly accuse the men Josh has worked for in China of having "lost" China because of their "Communist sympathies" and supposed treachery. Senator Joe McCarthy claims that the "Old China Hands" are spies and stooges for the Soviet Union. This new vocabulary of political discourse assumes enemies everywhere. And so the American government is purged of almost everyone who'd known and loved China. The experts are gone, the ship is rudderless. The Cold War is beginning to take shape.

Josh is too junior to have made any important decisions, and thus he avoids being brought down in the political crossfire. He is not fired from his job, nor called before the Congressional committee investigating Communists, unlike the higher-ranking men in the Embassy in Nanjing, or in the State Department, who were knowledgeable about the revolution that has swept China. The men he'd reported to.

Like thousands of other government employees, Josh is required to take a loyalty exam, and to have his family investigated should there be any Communists (real or imaginary) in his background. He is very, very careful about what he says. There's Josh's younger brother who's become a labor organizer and self-declared American Communist, and of course there's my whole family in "Red China." Government officials contact and question Josh, me, his colleagues and our friends, to judge whether we're "un-American" or perhaps even traitors. After stiff warnings and ironclad cautions, we're given a pass, no doubt partly because Josh was not sufficiently engaged in decision-making to be a political target.

Or, more likely, it was just because Josh's name wasn't on any of the reports that were sent from Nanjing to Washington. His colleague and good friend, Ed Martin, when asked how he'd escaped the widespread purge of experts on China, simply said: "because my name wasn't on any of the things I wrote. I wrote things, I'd submit them to someone else, Edmund Clubb or somebody else, and the thing would go out with their name on it, not mine." Josh has done the same. He's learned to erase himself while putting forward his views. He's learned to be very quiet—observant but quiet. He's learned to be cautious, always cautious.

I'm cautious too, now. I never talk politics, and anything I write is either anodyne or hidden.

However, Jim and Elaine, our closest friends from our days in Nanjing do not escape the purge. They are blind-sided when Jim—who was higher-ranking in the American Embassy in Nanjing—is told he can no longer work in government because of his work in "Red China" before the triumph of the People's Republic. Luckily Elaine has a job in Washington that will support them both, while Jim has to start from scratch in a new career. They have no children, and when they try to adopt a child they're informed by adoption agencies that their political views—based on his dismissal— make them ineligible to adopt. They begin a new life for themselves when Jim enters a PhD program while Elaine continues to work to support them both. We remain close friends with Jim and Elaine even as we're shocked at what's happened to Jim professionally. It's unheard-of for someone in their 40s to go back to school for a PhD. But having been tarred by congressional and other investigations, what choice does a China specialist have?

So this time, it's political riptides that sweep us away, not the war itself. The monstrous shape-shifting nightmare is now made real, and it's seemingly permanent. No more foolish hope. Now it's no longer war as we knew it. Now it's the Cold War, this new kind of war, a war of words and deterrents and threats and counter-threats. It's propaganda everywhere. It's obsession about spies and about the spread of nuclear weapons technology. Everywhere in Washington, the seat of government, there reigns fear about what can—and cannot—be said and written about China. It's illegal now to go to China. It's unthinkable to talk to anyone Chinese. A horrible orthodoxy descends on us. Now in America, anti-communism sweeps the land, the Cold War becomes our prison, and in it I see that I will never be able to return to China, that Peking and my family are lost to me forever.

CHAPTER 9

Cold War

After two years in Taipei, followed by another two years in Israel, we return to Washington, to deepfreeze Cold War surroundings compounded by 1950s race tension. The civil rights movement is gaining strength. Washington is a cauldron of political opposites on whether to grant equal rights to black citizens, called "Negroes" by themselves in that day. Sometimes our family of four attracts stares when we're together in public, on the street, onlookers wondering how we're related to one other, with my dark skin and ostentatiously Chinese dress (which just looks foreign to them, but that's the idea), Josh's fair looks, and Ann and Jean looking not even remotely related to one another.

Before one of our longer drives through Virginia to visit Colonial Williamsburg, Josh sits the girls down and tells them not to be upset if we're asked to leave a restaurant when we're in Virginia, "because some people don't understand families that look different." The girls are uncomfortable and mystified, but they seem game. Nothing to do but to see what happens.

Nothing happens. No one asks us to leave any restaurants. No one refuses us service. But the girls are learning this amorphous yet abrasive notion of race, something you have to learn to see, to feel, to intuit as an issue, as when you notice at Williamsburg that all the visiting people are white, and the serving people are black. No Chinese of course, no Asians. On most official forms, I'm still referred to as "yellow", but we don't mention that to the girls because none of us is actually yellow. So ridiculous. Not worth talking about.

In Williamsburg Josh takes pictures of statues, as he did in China so long ago. One picture shows the girls on either side of a Confederate general, probably Stonewall Jackson, and the girls have their arms linked through his. I think: this Civil War of theirs, so tame that even the losing side has built memorials to commemorate this war, to mark a way of life that still continues in certain ways that Josh and I can plainly see. The girls think it's just a bunch of creaky history you can brush aside. But they will discover that your history can't be tossed, because it's in your skin and your bones and the way your mind works, and it's acid to your feelings when they are crossed, crushed. Which is why we try never to dwell on race with the girls, because there's too much history and we don't want them cowed. We give briefings only when we think we must. Race comes at you from the outside but you don't let it stop you, you understand?

In Washington there are many blacks, but almost no Asians, few Chinese except diplomats and students and residents of a tiny Chinatown where I sometimes go in search of bean sprouts and tofu and *baotze*. No Asians in Boston either, when we visit Josh's parents there, except in their small Chinatown. I remain a curiosity to many who see me on the streets, but I can deal with this. I remind myself how in Peking we used to stare at some strange-looking foreigners, in fact how I stared at Josh when I first saw him at the library at Yenching so many years ago, but I was staring at his good looks, not his racial strangeness in China.

So I discuss race with my girls only when I have to. I don't want to make a big deal out of something I think they can handle just fine. Because they *have* to handle it just fine, no feeling sorry for themselves. When Ann comes to me in the kitchen to ask me if she's a "half-breed," I put down the carrots I'm peeling and I ask her where on earth she ever heard that word. She says she read it in one of her seventh-grade books about the wild west. I tell her it's not a nice word and never to use it. Done.

Another time the girls come home from school and say a kid recited a rhyme that goes like this:

Ching Chong Chinaman sitting on a fence
Trying to make a dollar out of fifteen cents
Along comes a policeman and bops him on the head
And that was the end of Ching Chong Chinaman.

This is stupid. In fact I tell them it's the stupidest thing I ever heard, and they need to understand that Chinaman isn't even a word. Just like Americaman isn't a word. Chinese people don't like being called Chinaman. They don't like being called Chinks, which is another bad word the girls might hear. Americans don't like being called gringos. These are not real words and it's pointless to use them. And that whole rhyme is just a stupid cartoon! End of lecturette.

I don't mention that it's even more stupid to say the Chinese can't do math, and downright shocking to hear a rhyme about being struck by police, all of this in a schoolyard ditty, but why dwell on it. Just move on. The girls have to be strong enough to ignore stupid stuff, that's all.

Around the same time, I take the girls to see the movie *South Pacific,* because I think this is the way to tell the girls about racial prejudice. The dashing American lieutenant gives up his "Tonkinese" girlfriend because she won't be accepted in Philadelphia or Princeton; but I think, ha, more likely he can't see marrying someone he has to do hand signals with, for god's sake, because they don't speak each other's languages. You can deal with that! Learn Tonkinese! And the part where the pretty American nurse hesitates to marry the wealthy French widower because he's been left with two (gasp) "Eurasian" children—well, I simply explain that the pretty nurse was just too old-fashioned, but she overcame that in the end. Happy ending.

So this is the way I try to deal with the difficulties of raising our two little girls in an America that isn't ready for mixed-race children. I try to make them feel comfortable and accepted, and that like me they can deal with it, because they just have to, no choice. (Where would it be any better? China? Just as bad about mixed-race.) So just *deal.* Prevail. Survive. I know these various kinds of situations will keep coming at them, all their lives. It's all harder than I'd imagined, but the girls do well in school and we stick together as a family. Ann is very shy of course, but Jean has a classroom full of friends, and her birthday parties are rollicking good times for the kids in her classroom, with Jean the life of the party. I think: we'll get by; we'll make this work.

School is where it's most important for things to work. I just tell them they must do well. I don't help them with homework unless they're completely stumped, which is never—because they have to learn to succeed without their parents, because they may lose their family the way I did. In life you never know. No time to waste, no time to be bored (what does that word even mean?), certainly no time for whining. Just do it, I always say.

And always see the positive. It's there, no matter what happens. I have no time for depression.

ONE EVENING AFTER THE GIRLS HAVE GONE TO BED, JOSH sits me down to give me news he's received. He doesn't tell me how he's received it, but it's a terrible blow: Po, my Concubine Grandmother, has died. She was my grandfather Liang Qichao's second wife, much younger, who initially worked as a handmaiden to my grandmother but then became concubine and second wife. She bore Liang Qichao six children who survived to adulthood, while my grandmother bore three who survived. That my grandfather had two wives at the same time, both of them having babies at the same time, was simply accepted at that time. Some men had four or five concubines. It was not unusual.

When I was a child, Po had always been far more sympathetic to me than my own mother ever was. She'd laugh at my stories, my sometimes zany ideas, and while my mother would just stare at me silently, Po would let mirth shake her, covering her mouth to hide her delight. She liked my independence, while my mother completely rejected it. In her own subtle way, back in 1939, Po had let me know that she understood my decision to leave China, to defy my mother, to flee the war, to marry Josh. She never held me morally responsible for my father's killing. The way she embraced me when I went to her that day, told me that she knew my self-accusing despair, my sense of guilt. Now she's gone: one of my cherished touchstones, one of the people I always thought about whenever I allowed myself to wonder how I'd fallen into exile from my homeland.

Of course, Josh and the girls are my first line of defense whenever doubts threaten to undermine me. I say almost nothing to the girls about Po's death, because they don't know about concubines and complicated Chinese families. But when I say "Po is gone," they look worried, so something must show on my face when I say the words. I turn to Josh for understanding.

But now Josh recedes. He recedes into his work. He tells me little or nothing of his work, because it's too dangerous in these days when politicians or even your colleagues might accuse you of being a Communist. Too many China experts have been purged or have had their reputations destroyed. He has a family to support, and he cannot afford to lose his job. And so a silence about his work settles over our family. A silence about anything political. The girls must not hear anything—nothing about the Soviet Union, nothing about China, nothing about their Chinese family, nothing about Communism (even omitting that Josh's brother is running for Congress on the American Communist Party ticket—he gets fewer than a thousand votes). Every time Josh sees this brother at, say, Thanksgiving dinner at his parents' home in Cambridge, he's required afterwards to file a report to the State Department declaring that no information was exchanged with his brother the American Communist. He doesn't tell the girls why it's dangerous to be a Communist, so they imagine skulduggery, and I have to tell them that's not the danger, and my vagueness about this, and about anything that's political, sets a pattern of staying quiet about whole swathes of life. Mystery shrouds our dinner table conversation whenever it veers towards family.

This is important when you consider the matter of the Communists in *my* family, my family in China. There's my cousin Sukie, who was beaten during the student march back in 1935 at the beginning of my story, who later went to Yan'an to join the Communist Party. During the civil war she went to California, but with the triumph of the People's Republic she returned to China with her husband. There's another cousin, plus an aunt, who are in the People's Liberation Army. There's my brother who's married to a Communist Party member. And there are other members of my very large extended family who have joined everyday Communist organizations, community and service organizations and various parts of the government. One of my uncles is an aerospace engineer at a research institute—and so forth. After all, China is now officially a Communist state, and to American eyes during the Cold War, that makes *all* their citizens Communists. I think: so simplistic, so uncomprehending.

Right now, the vast divide in American politics labels everything either Right or Wrong, Black or White, Communist or Anti-Communist, no degrees of gray. Because Josh works in the State Department, where colleagues are purged for being so-called Communist sympathizers, he must keep quiet about our complex family in the United States and in China, lest someone wrongly think he's being influenced by Communists, one of those silly accusations so carelessly thrown about and so cruelly used to fire people or to prosecute them. We can't communicate with anyone in my family in Peking: in these times it's unthinkable to write to "the enemy." With the children we're almost completely silent about family. They have no idea, almost zero information, about their Chinese grandmother, their cousins, and all the aunts and uncles. All my people might as well be dead to them. They're in the dark about what I've lost. It's better that way. No need to spread the sadness.

We live in silence about work also. I fill the silence with my stories, none of them political, all of them entertaining. At dinner, with the girls, we tell anecdotes. We never discuss politics or the things that are driving our family from one part of the world to another. I learn to live with silence and to fill the silence with my own words and my determined vivacity. My writing, which I now keep to myself, is mostly about childhood memories of Peking, completely nostalgic and devoid of the political. Years later I write about my time in Washington:

> *"When my daughters were still young enough for me to feed with fact or fancy as I pleased, I chose to forego, for the time being, my own China so that they might, with less confusion, learn of their father's America where, as Foreign Service children, they had lived all too little. For me, too, this was the easier course, for in learning of Boston, or of Washington, I could leave that Peking which existed no more. My husband had agreed with me all along that life in Peking as I had lived it was so complicated, and so removed* [Concubine Grand-mother!] *from a mid-century Washington suburb that any bits and pieces which might trickle out through the children's friends might be misunderstood or worse, be spun out as lies. Even to me, who truly lived those times, it all sounds, now, like a fairy-tale."*

Am I being paranoid? I don't think so. But we don't know now that Washington in the 1950s will later, in hindsight, come to seem as much a fairy-tale as Peking in the 1930s. All I know is that here, in the 1950s, the Washington fairy-tale ends badly for anyone who's knowledgeable about China.

I worry about Josh, this dashing, adventurous young explorer I met in Peking in another life, it seems. It's as though a light is going out in his heart, in his fierce curiosity to learn and to experience and to travel and to speak out. Or perhaps the light is being carefully hidden, in order (he thinks) to protect us all. He has a wife and children. He can't go back to university to finish his PhD, because there's no money for that. That road was not taken, and now it's too late, he thinks. I see he's lost the promise of the exciting career he thought he'd have, the promise that I'd wanted to share with him. He's lost the chance to be in China, and so have I.

Is Josh's career being held back because he has a Chinese wife? Very possibly. Competitors and career superiors who favor those who look like them and who went to the same schools as they did, would find me an easy target, by looks and (let's face it) by race. "She doesn't *look* American, so how can she represent the United States?" So, should I stop wearing Chinese clothing, stash away my *qipao* dresses? I'd still look foreign, because people here just *look* at an Asian-American and think "foreigner," never thinking we're Americans. Plus, I come from Peking, capital of the People's Republic of China.

No one ever says anything outright. I know of no promotions denied to Josh because of me. But in the 1950s and even the 1960s, having "a wife from Communist China" is not an asset. Josh cannot be an Ambassador—always my dream. He has to remain in the background.

How far we are from what we'd hoped for when we started out together! Almost every year of the 20 years since we first met has been driven by war or menaced by war. First the three years of separation by the Japanese invasion; and then two years of study as Germany and Japan ran amok; then, after Pearl Harbor, four years of demanding war work in Washington while World War II raged in both Europe and Asia. And then: the devastating four years in Nanjing, watching our dreams of a life in China slip beyond our grasp, and by grasp I'm not talking about reach, I'm talking about not understanding, not grasping, what has happened to us.

Now it's this different kind of war, the Cold War: Communism versus Democracy, or Communism versus Capitalism. We'd taken this war with us wherever we moved, and we'd moved quite often: to Taiwan, to Israel, then to Washington again. We'd thrashed around in a swamp of ideology, a constant battle of ideas, but ideas without flexibility, shouted by cold warriors who are deaf to anything good about China. There have been endless newspaper reports and television speeches and harangues about so-called traitors. I think: at least we don't have to deal with invading armies or hide under the bed from bombs dropped from the sky. At least this is only words.

YET THE WORDS DRIVE ACTIONS; THE WORDS CARRY THREATS. After nearly 10 years of silence I receive a message in a handwritten letter. The letter reaches me only after a twisted journey, handed off through multiple individuals in an effort to obscure its politically unacceptable origin: China. The letter tells me that my mother wants to hear from me because she is seriously ill. She has no phone, so if I respond I must write a letter.

But when I discuss this with Josh, we must wrestle with what to do. If I write to her, and the message is intercepted by the Chinese authorities (should they read the letter, and we're told that they always do), then they will know that my mother has a daughter who's in Washington. And we fear this could be very dangerous to my mother's entire family in Peking.

In addition, because Josh is at the State Department, for his wife to communicate with perceived Communists who are in China could cause him to be targeted by anti-communists in the U.S., such as the House Un-American Activities Committee (HUAC). He could be subpoenaed and then fired. It could be the end of his career.

Together we decide that I must not respond to my mother's plea. I understand this decision. Yet I think of those words from the Bible, "The Lord has blinded their eyes and hardened their hearts so that their eyes cannot see and their hearts cannot understand," and in some chamber of my soul I believe I've become a sinner. Yet I'd be committing an even greater sin were I to risk the physical safety of my mother and the family I've lost in Peking. Physical safety. Growing up in a war zone makes you think always first about *just staying alive.* I need to avoid bringing harm down on the heads of others. I would rather be a sinner than harm my family in Peking. But I've let down my mother, I've cut her down yet again, as I did when I first left Peking in 1939, and then again when I was forced out of China in 1949. This, the third time, is surely my last chance to reach her, and I do not. I cannot.

Before, I carried heartache about the choices I don't have. Now I suffer deep pain from the choice I do have.

CHAPTER 10

Ghosts of War

Even as we remain in the grip of the Cold War, and John F. Kennedy is elected president to "close the missile gap," and I'm surrounded by anti-communism, I think about the China I once knew. I'm not really cut out to be a Suburban Housewife, as we're called, though I've mastered that role too. So I write now simply to hold onto China. When the kids are in school, I try to capture the past. I'm careful, so careful, to stay away from politics. I write about life in China in my famous grandfather's home. I go to a writer's conference. I write to a magazine editor, proposing a series of articles. My letter sounds uncharacteristically timorous:

> *"Could you find some small use for the enclosed sliver of life? I am not a writer, and English is not native to me. Nevertheless, I feel that someone besides myself may enjoy a visit now and then to an authentic house and garden in a China long since lost. I consider myself well-adapted to US life. I participate, I cope.*
>
> *Still, many a situation can seem suddenly absurd to me. As long as I keep living I will encounter situations connecting me to roots in my past.*

Submerged in suburbia though I am, fragments of remembrance keep floating up. Some lie quite stagnant, dead debris. But others surge forth charged, insistent.

I would like to offer a first account in a series on life in the home of perhaps the greatest scholar-statesman of modern China (indeed some claim he was the most prolific and influential writer in the whole of Chinese history!) Just life and manners, no politics. If Austen in her "Pride and Prejudice" could avoid Napoleon, surely I can keep open-mindedness about Chiang and Mao. In fact, as the naturalized wife of a US Foreign Service Officer, I have to.

I hope this enclosure is enough to show you the form and tone I intend for each and for the whole, divided into individual titles. I can supply references, although I daresay no one will vouch for my memory or imagination...So let's call it Fiction, all except Grandfather who lives in every relevant history book. Look him up if you wish: Liang Qichao."

This seems safe, just talking about "life and manners." And I somehow think that because it's about Liang Qichao, surely the magazine will be interested. But I'm dead wrong. In America, no one's heard of Liang Qichao, beyond some university faculty here and there. He's just some obscure Chinese guy with an unpronounceable name, the editors say (but more politely). Will no one publish my endless memories of China?

Ten years pass, and here is what I'd really like to say, but I cannot ever send this to publishers, not today, not in these times of cold war. This is my private devastation, living in suburban America but remembering the *not*-cold wars, the hot and devastating wars I've seen and fled:

> "*There we sat in a luxury restaurant high above the Potomac, three well-groomed well-mannered Chinese ladies of indeterminate age, speaking Mandarin of the purest and most literary. We sipped teabag tea as we awaited lunch. 'What am I doing here?' I asked myself. 'Once I had a mother, but is she still living? If yes, where? Where are my brothers, once three. Cousins by the dozen. I am the only one not there. What am I doing here?'*
>
> "*Here in Washington, high from this restaurant, the Potomac flows slow and wide and shining. People prattle of pollution, of oil and detergents and plastic and tin.*
>
> "*I remember the Yangtze at highflood, when armies fought and government crumpled like an empty husk. I have watched a bloated buffalo hooked and dragged ashore, heard the gas escape as knives cut into the slimy mess for food. The whole of China, that spring by the river, was tossing wild as the grisly debris sliding down to the sea.*"

And this, in another memory:

> "*In a wide pedicab like a boat*
> *With prow blunted, open to the sea,*
> *Pushed into the waves of humans*
> *Swirling through the narrows*
> *Which serve as streets ...*

And like scavengers of the deep
Which crowd close to ship's bounty
Came the beggars, adrift,
With hands outstretched.
Others, God, Look, no hands,
Just sickness awash
From stumps without fingers,
Sticks without toes,
Breasts without succor,
Face without nose, Eyes without light,
Hearts without hope...
O do not ride by, Take heed of my white head,
My menfolk lie dead."

My agony slips out also in one of my short stories, a story that I don't send to anyone. It's about a man who returns from long years of war, to his wife, who's in their home but has become mute. He stays with her, but she never speaks, and eventually he asks his children what the reason is. They refuse to answer, until under enormous duress the youngest child, a boy, finally stammers out that their mother was killed by Japanese soldiers. It's only her ghost that the father's been with. At which point, in uncontrolled despair, he strangles that child.

I write in another story about a small boy from no one knows where, completely lost amid war:

"'What is your name?' she asks.
'Little Beetle.'

> 'No, no. Your family name.'
> 'Wang.'
> 'What is your village?'
> 'Wang-family Hamlet.'
> 'But where is it, she asks desperately.' There are thousands of Wang-family Hamlets.
> 'By a stream,' the boy answers eagerly. His eyes shine with memory. 'We swim in the stream—the fish glitter—my mother pounds the clothes on the bank. My mother—' His eyes fill with bewildered tears. He looks at us strangers, and starts to weep. It is not the weeping of a child."

After I write this story, I squirrel it away. I hide it. It is too political, too raw. So is this one:

> "And then I saw her, a very small child—thin, half-naked, crawling along the foot of the wall like a sick animal. She said nothing when I spoke to her. She made no noise. Just looked up into my face and panted. I took her up in my arms and carried her to the Red Cross.
> 'There are thousands of these,' they said bitterly. 'You would think the Japanese have no children.'
> They took her, of course, but she died that afternoon. There was nothing I could do for her except buy a tiny coffin and see her safely into the earth."

Behind these stories are also the ghosts of my family who have lost their lives in China, lost their lives to the invaders, during the long war and even after, family not buried, thrown to the winds, some doomed to walk forever, knowing no rest. But I write no more about these ghosts, or these shattered children, because they veil my perception and tear out my heart.

About other things I do write. Always I write. I have no idea whether my writing can ever be read, but I do not give up. If I cannot write to my family, and I cannot write for publication, then I will write for myself, alone. I know despair. I remember the wars. I remember Peking and I remember Nanjing.

Tomb Guardian

CHAPTER 11

Interregnum: Sishun's Story

When I write about the grisly water buffalo, the ghosts of the unburied dead, the remembered desperation, I do not know that my mother is already gone, that she'd died nearly five years before. No one has told me. This Cold War makes communication too risky, life-threatening, across that widening chasm in my nightmares, my family lost to me on the other side, now gone beyond hope.

But not beyond memory.

I learn about my mother's death only after the Cold War has begun to subside, when in 1972 an English friend who's recently traveled to China, sends me an undated letter from my brother Teddy railing against my brother Harold:

"Mother died in November 1966. She died utterly alone with no one by her side. I wasn't allowed to come; J.P. was also incapacitated, having been sent down (*xiafang*). Harold should have been there at Mother's death but he wasn't. I've decided never to speak to him again. He saw that Mother's remains were cremated and then knowing perfectly well there was a place for Mother in Father's vault he deliberately scattered Mother's ashes to the wind."

I can read no further. I carefully put the letter down on the coffee table. I walk to the kitchen, no, the bedroom, no, the terrace with the door closed behind me so no one will come. My mind has bent, my feelings warped, my nerves gone limp—and then suddenly I'm steeled. I must not cry.

I say to myself: what did you expect? Did you expect of your mother an immortality to match endless war? Of course not. People die. I clench my hands until they cripple.

My mother Sishun died during the early stages of the massive upheaval of the Cultural Revolution. China has gone through difficult times since our time in Nanjing. If my mother died alone, then I know she died in pain. I know. And though I try to tell myself another story, I eventually learn more about her death. This is what's haunted me my whole life.

I need to tell you this story, my mother's ineffably sad story, because she walks alone to this day. She's not a ghost in the western sense, but a presence who needs to be acknowledged. There have been ceremonies for the beloved dead in my family, virtually all with graves or at least a memorial plaque. But for my mother? Nothing. She who believed so deeply in Chinese tradition has been abandoned in her death, stripped of recognition, no grave for her family to visit, to honor, to sweep each April. In the China I knew, those who are unburied still walk. Because of political turmoil, my mother had no recognition, no burial, and thus she stirs in my mind, no escape.

BORN IN PEKING THE ELDEST CHILD OF THE FAMOUS reformer Liang Qichao, my mother was named Liang Sishun 梁思顺, the last character meaning "to obey, to follow." That is what she did: she obeyed her father, and she obeyed the traditional Chinese strictures of family. In family pictures, you can see Sishun evolving from a graceful and slightly rounded teenager in a high-collared Chinese tunic and long skirt, to a 45-year old widow wearing a strict black *qipao,* with stern mouth and erect posture, thin enough to seem shriveled. In her 60's, in what's now the People's Republic of China, she's wearing plain black trousers and loose shirt, a Chinese working elder, but the way she sits is regal, shoulders thrown back, elegant. She still rules her family, but for me.

But I'm getting ahead of myself.

When she was five, Sishun's father was forced to flee from the Empress' beheading order, taking hasty refuge in Japan. Sishun and her mother later joined him in exile, accompanied by the handmaiden who became her father's concubine (and his second wife)—my "Concubine Grandmother," or *Po.* Supposedly my grandmother, his first wife, approved of this. Po was seventeen when she became Liang's concubine, only seven years older than Sishun.

Is it any surprise that Sishun disliked Po? She wanted to be loyal to her own mother. And there were territorial issues between Sishun and Po. Plus, Sishun's mother, a delicate beauty, was from a well-to-do family and was considered highly intelligent and knowledgeable. By contrast, Po's origins were unknown, because she'd been a child of peasants, had been adopted several times, and was illiterate when she became Liang's concubine, though later she learned to read. Sishun, who became so educated that she grew to be her father's intellectual alter ego, looked down on Po.

Sishun's mother bore two more surviving children, while Po bore six who survived. Thus, Liang Qichao had nine children who lived to adulthood. Sishun was the oldest child by far, and because she was so much older, she helped both her mother and Po to raise all the little ones surrounding them. Po continued to bear children into the 1920s, so Sishun's own children (including me) were the same ages as her younger half-siblings. And Sishun helped to raise them all: her own children and her father's, from both his wives. The generations blurred.

Over and over, Sishun knew grief. She saw four of the family's children die before adulthood, and several more stillborn. Three of the children died in a single episode, the typhoid epidemic in 1923. Having helped to raise them, it had felt as though these lost children were her own. Nine years later, one of Sishun's young half-brothers, who was trained at West Point, died in Shanghai in the early part of the fight against the Japanese invasion. He was in the 19th Route Army, only 25 years old, strikingly handsome. I was a teenager then, and I'd thought him the best-looking man I'd ever seen. I think I mourned his loss even more than my mother did. Po, his mother, had wailed her heartbreaking loss, but my mother Sishun was utterly silent in her grief for her half-brother.

Less than five years later, to Sishun's dismay, one of her half-sisters left college to join the Communist Party forces in Yan'an. Another joined the New Fourth Army. These were the two half-sisters (technically aunts, to me) who in age were only a year apart from me, and we three little girls had played together in the courtyards of home, under the benign eye of Po—who in truth I loved deeply, perhaps more than my own mother, I confess.

To westerners I referred to Po as "Concubine Grandmother", even though westerners think of concubines as mistresses. So, in order not to confuse (or shock) my western friends, I nearly always referred to Po's sons and daughters as my "cousins," even though they were actually my aunts and uncles. Nearly all of them were around my age, or even younger, and only one insisted always that I call him "Uncle" (a recognition that although I'm ten years older, I'm a generation behind). True enough.

Family rank: westerners sometimes just roll their eyes in exasperation, and maybe that's what I want them to do. I'm complicated, unusual; and this serves to remind them. I tell people my convoluted family is a Chinese thing, and they never get it, but westerners are allowed to be wrong about these things, whereas other Chinese have to get it right, absolutely right. We're sticklers about ancestry!

So Sishun, my mother, probably saw that I was closer to Po than to her, and to her it was all wrong for her daughter to be so influenced by her father's concubine. Plus, it must have hurt her. How could it not? She'd attended to the raising of all her siblings and half-siblings, as well as her own children, so perhaps she couldn't help but be stern, full of rules, even cold. In my memory, my mother never reached for me, never hugged me.

Maybe her life was just too hard, too emotionally difficult for her to show love. She'd prevailed over abrupt changes, deeply wounding setbacks, deaths and near-deaths, yet always sticking to the rules and the high expectations of her famous father. Perhaps this is why she had no patience with those who objected to what was expected of them. With her younger siblings and especially with her own children, she had no use for complaints or even differing opinions. She was judgmental. She said I was *lihai,* fierce and stubborn but foolish. It seemed that being well-behaved was more important to her than love. Later, but only when it was too late, I learned that she did love.

Sishun worked tirelessly for her father, my grandfather, until his death in 1929. She was Liang Qichao's closest intellectual colleague, his sounding-board for the last 35 years of his professional life. She did research for his famous essays on politics, editing and exchanging thoughts with him directly, or by mail when he traveled or she was abroad. Over the years he wrote hundreds of letters to his beloved Sishun, seeking her opinions and delivering his own. She matched his intellect in a way that made her his closest companion. She also developed an expertise on Chinese classical poetry, and wrote poetry herself. Liang encouraged her in this, seeing his eldest child as gifted in creativity as well as analysis. He admired her talent for languages as she mastered English and Japanese and later Russian, in addition to several Chinese dialects.

But Sishun was always expected to hew to his wishes. She never strayed. She was rigid. She was obedient, and she expected her children to be so.

Her father grew in political stature. He continued to publish and to speak about China's role in history, and the need for China to regain its sovereignty, lost to western powers and to Japan. In 1903 he'd traveled to America to raise funds for the new China of his hopes. His interests were wide-ranging and he was generous in spirit. Not only seeking money for political causes in China, once he even gave a fundraising speech in New York's Chinatown to raise money from Chinatown residents to help Jews fleeing the pogroms of Russia. He met with Theodore Roosevelt (who was more impressed by Japanese military might than by Chinese reform efforts). Liang traveled by train to Syracuse, Chicago, Los Angeles, and other parts of America to give his speeches for China.

He was forward-thinking in other ways too. When Sishun reached the age when little girls were often forced to have their feet bound with tight, bone-crushing cloth to meet a century-old standard of Chinese beauty, Liang rejected this cruelty. My mother was allowed to grow up with natural feet. They were called big feet, but they were only size 5, like my feet. Sishun was the model for big feet for all the little girls who were born after her in the Liang household.

I FOCUS ON ALL THIS BECAUSE MY MOTHER GREW UP IN A sprawling family rich not only in its history, but in the sheer number of people around her, with many children, many other family members, many guests, and many servants living in a multi-courtyard residence that served for working and living, schooling and play—and always, always surrounded by the sound of voices in talk and jest and argument.

But she died completely alone, without any of her sons present and without knowing that her long-gone only daughter had lived to love her after all.

I brush aside tears now, pressing on to tell more of my mother's story. Her father Liang Qichao had selected her future husband, and she'd dutifully married his choice: Zhou Guoxian, an assistant to Kang Youwei, the other reformer who'd escaped beheading. This was an arranged marriage, but a successful one. Her father took credit. Guoxian was ten years older, but Sishun liked his fierce patriotism, his pride in all things Chinese, his fearless stride, his canny ability to make money. Her father had insisted, against custom, that the wedding be at the Liang family home—the bride's home, not the groom's. Thus the groom (not letting this irregularity pass unremarked) arrived with swagger in a "decorated sedan chair," no doubt red and gold. Guoxian was not to be pushed around.

Thus Sishun lived in the shadow of two very strong men, my grandfather and my father, and both of them died too young. With the death of my grandfather, China lost a distinguished leader and my mother lost her work as his researcher and intellectual companion. With the death of my father, my mother may have lost part of her compass, no one left to obey or to follow. She lived her last nearly thirty years without remarrying. In Chinese tradition, this was considered the most honorable course of action.

In the matter of honor, Sishun was as tough as Guoxian. After his death, when Japanese soldiers appeared at her doorstep, she dressed them down with stern warnings not to seize her belongings, her words uttered in impeccable court Japanese of the highest class. Gobsmacked, the soldiers left. Later, she refused entreaties to accept positions in Chiang Kai-shek's Nationalist government, a government she could never support. Toward false authority as well as toward family, she turned a stern face, a withering stare.

My mother and father had four children. I was the oldest, and the only daughter. Sishun and we children had traveled with our father Guoxian to his diplomatic postings in southeast Asia and Canada, and these must have been the halcyon years for my mother. But in late 1928 Liang Qichao's health sharply declined, and Sishun rushed home to her father. Too late. Liang died in 1929. In 1931 the Japanese began their long invasion by seizing Manchuria. In 1937 they conquered Peking. My father had become a law professor, and he withheld support for the Nationalist government of occupied Peking, refusing also to cooperate with the Japanese conquerors. So you see, it's no accident that I held these views also, and that I'd marched in that December 9th demonstration in only my second year of college.

But my mother Sishun didn't believe in public demonstrations. She was opposed to strident voices. She believed women, especially young women, have no business getting involved in political matters. And then she discovered, to her fury, that her only daughter, so very unlike her, had decided to rebel. That daughter wrote dangerously strident pamphlets against the Japanese invader. She fell under the influence of Lin Huiyin, an independent spirit with insufficient regard for tradition, in Sishun's view. More, her daughter socialized with intellectuals full of dangerous ideas, and she seemed to have successive boyfriends. And then she chose her own husband—unthinkable in itself—and far worse, that choice was "a blue-eyed boy," a westerner, someone from another race, another culture, another country across a vast ocean.

That rebellious daughter was Zhou Nianci, calling herself Nancy Zhou, who defied her parents with the words "I'm not afraid of making my *own* choices." Unthinkable choices.

Sishun loses me, her only daughter, to that *waiguoren,* that American. Nothing for years, and then in the ninth year a short visit from her daughter, and she's given a glimpse of Nianci's two little girls, the younger only 6 months old. And then never again. She never sees them again. She's never told why, though she can guess. She searches the newspapers and asks everyone who might know of Nancy, *Nianci*. She writes letters that never see delivery. She waits for information, any small scrap, and it never comes.

––––

IT GETS WORSE. BECAUSE MY MOTHER IS AN INTELLECTUAL and the widow of a professor and diplomat, she's designated a class enemy, part of "the Stinking Ninth Class" of enemies.

She becomes a target during the Cultural Revolution that threw China into that "chaotic decade". Some Red Guards strong-arm their way into her home and destroy many of her papers. Fortunately, most of her father's papers—Liang Qichao's writings—are rescued. But my mother suffers interrogation, forced labor, denial of medicine, and even beatings. From lauded heights she's descended into a morass of social upheaval, seeing zealots destroy the literature, research, and ancient objects that were the very underpinning of the traditions she'd upheld all her life.

I close my eyes and I see her staggering, trying to stand upright amidst hurricane winds, her body leaning fearfully into the onrush, still stoic, determined to be strong.

Now falling seriously ill, her feelings unloosed, she cries out for her daughter, sending messages by way of Canada. A letter sent by a close friend of hers says this:

> "Liang Sishun's health has been very poor lately. She has had heart disease for a long time. Every time she writes she says she doesn't have much time left and her tone is very despondent. If we can receive a letter from Nancy comforting her mother, there would be nothing better for her spirits. Even if we can't get a letter from her, if we can know some news about her current life, that would make her mother very happy too. I've heard that the degree to which Liang Sishun misses her daughter is heartbreaking."

Still she hears nothing, not a hint. She grows old. The deprivations have taken a toll. The silence stretches long and it lasts to her death, her death during that time of upheaval when two sons have been sent to remote provinces and the third seems afraid of his shadow. She wonders about her fear-less daughter, the one who stepped off a cliff, now 27 years ago, in pursuit of something called "true love" and with a steamer ticket to escape the invading Japanese. Where is that daughter? Her granddaughters? Are they safe? Are they happy? Nianci, Nianci, was it worth it to give up your family? Was your "own choice" the right choice?

Oh Christ, that it were possible
For one short hour to see
The souls we loved,
That they might tell us
What and where they be

—Alfred Lord Tennyson

[Jotted on the back of a photo of Sishun's brother in uniform. Nianci's closest uncle, he was killed during a Japanese attack on Shanghai. It's unclear whether the handwriting is Sishun's or Huiyin's.]

CHAPTER 12

War's End

J osh is at the State Department, focusing on Southeast Asia. It's 1972. The Cold War has been thawing, melting away so fast that we lose our bearings. I'm astonished that the president of the United States—the very one who as a young politician had made his name by accusing Josh's colleagues of being "soft on Communism"—has flown to Peking and has shaken hands with Mao Zedong himself. Unthinkable things stare out at us from our TV as we sit nightly to watch the news while sipping iced drinks. Our world tilts. Our lives, so long driven by the Cold War, are coming unhinged, as a door that was firmly closed and locked seems suddenly to have fallen away. Splintered. Discarded. Flat on the ground. Could we have lived our whole lives so warped by politics now so suddenly tossed away? Was China so near after all?

Nearly 25 years of silence! Friends and family dead or scattered. Peking a wraith or a monolith, depending on whom you're talking to. I'm distraught, damaged, corroded by deep suspicion of lost opportunity. I return to my desk and I write my turmoil, a howling nostalgia.

"WHY IS MY PEKING SO STILL?

Word by word

Gray stones dug from cold ruins

News of the U.S. visitation

Sluiced and slid

Like slag

To slump in heaps

Gross and dead.

I delve deep

Hopeful of buried treasure

Of colors remembered,

Of shimmer and sheen

Elusive, faint.

None! How is this possible!

More than any other

Peking is a place of sounds.

No news. None!

No word of the thousand sounds

Which <u>must</u> enwrap

The people of my city

Sounds that sting or soothe

The ears of all but the deaf.

How can Peking be so still?

Where are the simple sounds

Of basic life

Which so enchanted Polos three
And just a few years ago
Me, grown
Of such living
How, now, this eerie choke
This silent smother of vibrant fire
First, on a winter day
When the sun freezes gold
Above sparkling roofs
Of green or yellow
Or soft gray.
Where are the pigeons?
Birds that wheel and fan and dip
In the diamond blue
Of sky, so high,
Spinning from bamboo flutes
Tied to feathers.
Strong wires of tone
Now taut, now slack,
Weaving a canopy of sound
To cover a whole city
Which can only be Peking.
On earth below
A sweet echo,

From children wheeling diabolos
Back and forth
On strings tied
Between two sticks
One in each hand,
Diabolos which transported, fell silent
In the hands of inept jugglers
In the court of France
But sing at ease like flutes
For the children of Peking
Where are those diabolos?? . . . . .
. . . .
. . . .

At last in deepest night
In wind or rain
Or in the still of snow or moon
Comes the street-watch.
Plock, plock, plock
With his stick and block
With comfort threefold
To soften the edge of sleep.
'The heart feels content,
Family gathers whole.
City rests in peace.'
Where is the street-watch

With his little red block?

Plock, plock, plock."

Here's the hard, bitter core of what's happened. My Peking is no longer forbidden, but it's gone. The street-watch is gone: my family will never gather whole, my heart feels never content. The edge of sleep is not soft, it's hard; it slashes. And these ghosts: did I strangle a loved one? Do ghosts walk this world? *Quan jia tuan yuan, meiyou.*

NOW JOSH AND I LIVE IN RETIREMENT IN WHAT SEEMS TO me a plastic community in Florida. However, as always, we make many friends and I spend most of my days continuing my writing, the writing that's sustained me throughout my life. By now, I've written and rewritten hundreds of pages of short stories and memoirs and poetry based on my years of childhood and youth in Beijing—everyone now says Beijing, no more Peking, but I still think Peking. The pages have been lovingly edited and re-edited, my handwriting and jottings improving each draft. My heart is in those pages. The meaning of my life is in those pages.

"ON VIEWING EMBROIDERY WROUGHT ON GAUZE BY A LADY IN HUNGARY

The fabric of my life spreads plain for all to see,

Of texture firm and pattern set

In line and curve and hue.

No matter the weave, now dense now loose,

Of gossamer thin of light and shade.

Suppose one day I add a thread

Of wondrous strength and shine

And strive to twist with skill of head and hand

Its vibrant pulse, to make it one

With what has long lain waiting.

One stitch or two, one plume, one curl,

And upward leaps to catch my heart

New shapes, new molds, fresh links and chains,

Rare locks and keys which free or fetter

Inside this maze called Life.

This thread was made I know for other use.

I can but try to draw it close.

If it hangs frayed, in knots, misused by some

To patch in vain rude rents in their worn lives,

I still would try to put to fuller use.

I can but try, in brief, to smooth ruined strands,

And use its gleam to warm, to light

Through time and space and silence

My papered words, my trove of thought and feeling

Which now has long lain fading."

The thread I want to add is my writing. With a twist it creates new shapes, fresh links. It pulls together my life, however frayed. It's "my papered words, my trove of thought and feeling." And I see it fading.

I keep trying. I send samples of my short stories to editors, publishers. I ask friends for contacts in the publishing world, and I buttonhole people at dinner parties. People respond warmly, but I'm told my writing is either too painterly ("not enough plot") or the plot is too strange. Probably they mean too Chinese (traditions, concubines, ghosts, spirits)—not that anyone actually says that. My descriptions of how we used to live speak of something now vanishing into air, the thinnest sheer of memory. The world, always in a hurry, just barrels through the sheer as though it weren't there at all. The world looks to the future. No one's interested in looking back. But back is where I come from, who I am, who I'll always be.

Now one of my brothers, J.P., who's been a professor at a university in Beijing, comes to the U.S. for a year of research. He flies to Miami and when Josh and I meet him at the airport, I see my kid brother for the first time since he was a teenager. He's an old man now, stooped by three decades and by abuse and deprivation during the now-past chaotic decade (I learn that he never uses the term Cultural Revolution). We barely embrace—close hugs or even *any* hugs are not in my family or in our culture—but what I see is the teenage kid I left behind, the kid now old, and I start to weep for all that we've lost. But I catch myself; I don't allow myself to break down.

When we return from the airport and have had tea on the patio—a far cry from the courtyards and the moon gate of our family home in Peking—he gives us news of family. He tells us that after some scattering during the chaotic decade, my extended family are now largely in Beijing again. Some were lost to mistreatment and illness and suicide, he says. Some never received a full education because of the chaotic decade, and thus they have little training and speak little or no English.

Most painful of all, we speak of the hellish deaths of our parents, our father suddenly cut down by Japanese soldiers, our mother attacked and dying at the outset of the chaotic decade. The memory of these losses never goes away. Like a stubborn cinder in the eye, the truth scrapes hard, it waters our vision, and yet we cannot dwell on it. After all, we're Chinese. But in my heart I know that twice I failed to answer our mother in her hour of need. Such were the demands of the Cold War, but who am I kidding? She died alone, unprotected, her daughter at far remove, none of her three sons present. Worse, she was never buried: Sishun's ashes, which should have been placed at my father's tomb, were simply disposed of. By upbringing I know her ghost still walks, and J.P. knows it too, but like so much of our lives we cannot speak of it. We will it away.

Then I call up my courage and I tell my brother about my writing, the writing of these long decades of exile (but I never use that word). I tell him how wherever Josh and I went, and however unpredictable and interrupted the circumstances, I always had my writing. I was always able to carry Peking in my head and in my heart.

My words rush forth—it's been decades since I've spoken with anyone who's living in Beijing, and my joy is unbounded. He agrees to read my work, at least some of my stories (how could he refuse?). I practically run to my study and come back with a pile of the stories, typed pages with my handwritten edits and second thoughts. J.P. smiles good-naturedly and jokes that this will at least help him fall asleep once he retires to bed.

———————

NEXT MORNING DAWNS WITH THE USUAL STARING BRIGHT-ness of a Florida day, and I eagerly seek my brother. I find J.P. already up and sitting on the patio with a mug of tea steaming in his grasp, gazing out at palm trees in sunshine. He doesn't look happy.

"J.P., did you sleep well? Probably too well, if you tried to read my stories," I joke, weakly. "What did you think of them?"

And this is the moment I can never forget:

J.P. carefully puts down his tea and sits there looking down at his feet. "Nianci, you can't publish these, you just can't," he says.

No preamble, no gentle let-down, just hits me with this statement. I stare at him and I know my eyes are stunned because when he glances up he can't meet them.

"It's too risky," he continues, "our family has gone through too much. If you publish this, then everyone will know that we have a sister who's married to an American who was in Washington on the wrong side of the Cold War. It will bring more trouble to our family in Beijing, and we've only just come through the chaotic decade."

"But the Cold War is practically over!" I can feel my face flushing, my hand shaking so much that I have to put down my tea also.

"It isn't over," he says. "We can't be sure, we can never be sure. You can never publish these stories. Not if you care about your family. Not at all. I am sorry."

He gets up and goes back to the guest room and closes the door. For all I know, he is crying too. Because now I am crying. I weep as I seldom do, in fact never do. I shudder, I wrack, I break down. I know now that I'll never have a voice. My losses stay mute. And the Peking I've written about for so many years stays lost.

I want you to understand how the Peking I left behind is always with me. I cannot lose China. I make sure that my daughters understand this, and their children too. Of course my daughters are Americans. But not truly American. China is in them, in their heads and in their bones. They cannot escape China any more than I can return to the Peking I came from. I left, I went back, and then I was torn away forever.

ACKNOWLEDGMENTS

My deepest debt is to my husband, Richard Bowers, who encouraged me throughout this journey, and who often edited my work with a sharp eye for detail and nuance. Without Rick, this book would still be enroute.

My children and daughter-in-law were on the receiving end of several drafts, and offered important support over many, many months. Marya Spence, my younger daughter who's an exceptionally talented literary agent, was able to provide particularly knowledgeable advice.

Friends and colleagues, near and far, read earlier drafts, often advising and always encouraging. There is no way to overstate how much I appreciate their views. I want especially to acknowledge comments from Bettina and Craig Burr, Josh (Jiashu) Cheng, Richard Chow, David deWilde, Gail Edie, Bev Freeman, Arar Han, Eugenie Havemeyer, Lonnie Hinchey, Carma Hinton, Erica Johnson, Julie Kidd, Diana Lary, Andrew Levy, Mengxi Li, Fenrong Liu, Susan Morris, Bart Rocca, Joseph Seeley, Iven Sha, Marieke Spence, Jim Stone, Chao Fen Sun, Henry and Meredith Von Kohorn, Bingyi Wang, and Nora Wu.

Nora Wu, whose family history paralleled mine in certain respects, was especially encouraging, urging me to bring my mother's story forward. Prof. Diana Lary of the University of British Columbia, whose expertise on China during the years of invasion by Japan is deep and longstanding, took the trouble to read and comment on an earlier draft. Mengxi Li brought critical skills in translating writings and documents concerning and by Zhou Nianci, Liang Qichao (including classical Chinese), and others. Joseph Seeley conducted thorough web research in Chinese. Carma Hinton, noted documentary filmmaker, guided me not only on Chinese usage, practices, art, and mythology, but also on design choices for the book. Gail Edie and Susan Morris offered detailed and trenchant commentary at an early stage. I'm grateful also to Fenrong Liu, who urged me to publish this story, because it gives unusual insight into how the complex conditions in Peking and Nanjing affected individual lives, including some in Liang Qichao's family.

Not least, I'm indebted to Stanford University where, during two years as a Fellow at the Distinguished Career Institute (DCI Fellow), I was able to initiate and pursue the background research necessary for this book, even partially regaining the Chinese language I'd lost years earlier. Further, the Stanford Center at Peking University, where in October 2019 I was a Visiting Researcher, played an extraordinarily important role. The Center is located in Beijing, on the Beijing Daxue (Beida) campus, the very campus where my parents met in 1936, at the start of the story in *Nancy|Nianci*. For the honor and opportunity to have pursued my research at Beida, I am deeply grateful to Jean Oi, Professor of Political Science at Stanford University and the Director of the Center; and to Josh Cheng, Executive Director. I was working at Beida on the 70th anniversary of the founding of the Peoples Republic of China, a date that was meaningful in this book, *Nancy|Nianci*.

Finally, I'm enormously grateful to Holly Fairbank, who gave me access to the Wilma Cannon Fairbank papers at the Peabody Essex Museum Archives. There I was able to read the letters of my great-aunt, Lin Huiyin, to Wilma and John Fairbank. Also included were some letters and notes from Zhou Nianci, my mother, and from other Chinese who were enduring the wars. Above all, Holly gave me encouragement to pursue my mother's story, as she has so carefully preserved her own parents' legacy.

PUBLISHED SOURCES

Auden, W.H. and Christopher Isherwood, *Journey to a War* (Random House, 1939)

Ballard, J.G., *Empire of the Sun* (Simon and Schuster, 1984)

Baschet, Eric, *China 1890-1938: From Warlords to World War, a History in Documentary Photographs* (Jeunesse Verlagsanstalt Vaduz, 1989)

Biggerstaff, Knight, *Nanking Letters 1949* (East Asia Program, Cornell University, 1979)

Carey, Arch, *The War Years at Shanghai: 1941-45-48* (Vantage Press, 1967)

Chang, Gordon H. *Friends and Enemies: The United States, China, and the Soviet Union 1948-1972* (Stanford University Press, 1991)

Chang, Gordon H., "Trans-Pacific Composition: Zhang Shuqi Paints in America," in *Zhang Shuqi in California* (Silicon Valley Asian Art Center, 2011)

Clough, Marshall S., *Until We Meet Again: An American Woman and Her Family in Civil War China* (Walden Press, 2020)

Dawes, James, *Evil Men* (Harvard University Press, 2013)

Department of State, *Peace and War: United States Foreign Policy 1931-1941* (U.S. Government Printing Office, 1942)

Doglia, Arnaud, "Japanese Mass Violence and its Victims in the Fifteen Years War (1931-45)," SciencesPo (École Libre des Sciences Politiques, Paris) Research Network, 2011

Fairbank, John King, *Chinabound: A Fifty-Year Memoir* (Harper & Row, 1982)

Fairbank, Wilma C., *Liang and Lin: Partners in Exploring China's Architectural Past* (University of Pennsylvania Press, 1994)

Finnane, Antonia, "Changing Spaces and Civilized Weddings in Republican China," in *New Narratives of Urban Space in Republican Chinese Cities,* edited by Billy K.L. So and Madeleine Zelin (Brill, 2013)

Flath, James, and Norman Smith, *Beyond Suffering: Recounting War in Modern China* (University of British Columbia Press, 2011)

French, Paul, *Midnight in Peking: How the Murder of a Young Englishwoman Haunted the Last Days of Old Peking* (Penguin Books, 2013)

Hobart, Alice Tisdale, *Oil for the Lamps of China* (Bobbs-Merrill, 1933)

Jespersen, T. Christopher, *American Images of China, 1931-1949* (Stanford University Press, 1996)

Jia, Sophie Site, "Sun Yatsen, Liang Qichao: Friends, Foes and Nationalism" (article published by Emory University, 2015)

Jowett, Philip, *China and Japan at War 1937-1945: Rare Photographs from Wartime Archives* (Pen & Sword Books, 2016)

Kaplan, Lawrence M., *Homer Lea: American Soldier of Fortune* (The University of Kentucky Press, 2010)

Kwan, Michael David, *Things That Must Not Be Forgotten: A Childhood in Wartime China* (Soho Press, 2000)

Lary, Diana, *China's Civil War: A Social History 1945-1949* (Cambridge University Press, 2015)

Lary, Diana, "Memory Times, Memory Places: Public and Private Memories and Commemoration of the Resistance War in China (Keynote delivered at the International Workshop, "Asia's 'Great War": Memories and Memoryscapes of the 1937-1945 Conflict," University of Essex, 22 March 2014)

Lary, Diana and Stephen MacKinnon (editors), *Scars of War: the Impact of Warfare on Modern China* (University of British Columbia Press, 2001)

Lee, Sophia, *Yanjing University 1937-1941: Autonomy or Compromise* (University of Tulsa, 1980)

Liang, Qichao, letter dated 1915 to his eldest child Liang Sishun (mother of Zhou Nianci), giving his eldest grandchild the name *Nianci*, along with the nickname *Gui'er* or "Little Cinnamon"

Liang, Sili, *The Story of a Rocket Designer*, translated into English by Andrew Niu, 2008

Liao, C.S., *Cheng-Fu Wang: A Visionary Industrialist and Fungbin Liu Wang: An Undaunted Humanist* (Wang Family 1978)

Lindsay, Michael, *The Unknown War: North China 1937-1945* (Bergstrom & Boyle Books, 1975)

Melby, John F., *The Mandate of Heaven: Record of a Civil War, China 1945-49* (University of Toronto Press, 1968)[1]

Miller, Alice Lyman and Richard Wich, *Becoming Asia: Change and Continuity in Asian International Relations Since World War II* (Stanford University Press, 2011)

Mishra, Pankaj, *From the Ruins of Empire: The Revolt Against the West and the Remaking of Asia* (Picador, 2012)

Mitter, Rana, *Forgotten Ally: China's World War II 1937-1945* (Houghton Mifflin Harcourt 2013)

New York Historical Society, *Chinese American Exclusion/Inclusion* (Scala Arts Publishers, 2014)

Peck, Graham, *Two Kinds of Time* (University of Washington Press, 1950 and 2008)

Qiu, Peipei (with Su Zhiliang and Chen Lifei), *Chinese Comfort Women: Testimonies from Imperial Japan's Sex Slaves* (Oxford University Press, 2014)

Reuther, David, "Interview: Ambassador Darryl Norman Johnson" (The Association for Diplomatic Studies and Training, Foreign Affairs Oral History Project, March 26, 2006)

Rosenbaum, Arthur Lewis, *New Perspectives on Yenching University, 1916-1952* (Brill, 2012)

---

1   The quote from the "Embassy observer" on page 107 is from this text.

Salisbury, Harrison, *China: 100 Years of Revolution* (Holt, Rinehart & Winston, 1983)

Schaller, Michael, *The U.S. Crusade in China, 1938-1945* (Columbia University Press, 1979)

Schlesinger, Marian Cannon, *San Bao and His Adventures in Peking* (Gale Hill Books, 1935, 1998; description of daily life in Peking, based on her 1934 year-long visit)

Seligman, Scott D. "The Night New York's Chinese Went Out for Jews: Looking Back at an Unlikely Collaboration in 1903," (*Jewish Daily Forward,* February 4, 2011)

Slack, Edward R., Jr., *Opium, State, and Society: China's Narco-Economy and the Guomindang, 1924-1937* (University of Hawaii Press, 2001)

Smedley, Agnes, *Battle Hymn of China* (Alfred A. Knopf, 1945)

Snow, Helen Foster, *My China Years* (William Morrow & Company, 1984)[2]

Snow, Lois Wheeler, *Edgar Snow's China: A Personal Account of the Chinese Revolution Compiled from the Writings of Edgar Snow* (Random House, 1981)

Stuart, John Leighton, *Fifty Years in China* (Random House, 1954)

Tan, Amy, *Where the Past Begins: Memory and Imagination* (Harper Collins, 2017)

Tata, Sam, and Ian McLachlan, *Shanghai 1949: The End of an Era* (New Amsterdam, 1989)

Tretiakov, S., translator, *A Chinese Testament: The Autobiography of Tan Shih-Hua* (Simon and Schuster, 1934)

Tuchman, Barbara W., *Notes from China* (Random House, 1972)

Tuchman, Barbara W., *Stilwell and the American Experience in China 1911-45* (MacMillan Publishers, 1971)

---

2   The quote from the "wife of an American journalist" [Edgar Snow] on page 6 is from this text.

van de Ven, *China at War: Triumph and Tragedy in the Emergence of the New China* (Harvard University Press, 2018)

Wang, Chi-chen, Editor, *Stories of China at War;* includes authors Kuo Mo-Jo, Mao Dun, Lao She, Chang Tien-yi (Columbia University Press, 1947)

Wang, K.P., *A Chinese-American Exciting Journey Into the 21st Century* (AuthorHouse, 2006)

West, Philip, *Yenching University and Sino-Western Relations, 1916-1952* (Harvard University Press, 1976)

Wu, Liming, *Liang Qichao he ta de er nü men* (Beijing University Press, 2009, 2006, 2001)

Zhang, Ailing (Eileen Chang), *Love in a Fallen City* (University of Hong Kong, 1996)

Zhang, Ailing (Eileen Chang), *Lust, Caution* (Anchor Books/ Random House, 2007)

In addition: Articles from English-language newspapers published in Peking and Shanghai

Nanjing, 1947

ABOUT THE AUTHOR

Bian An (卞 安) is both the given name and pen name of Ann Bennett Spence, who was raised by a Chinese mother and an American father in China, the US, and other countries. Until school age she spoke only Chinese. In adulthood, after Wellesley College, she went on to East Asian studies at Harvard and a Stanford MBA, followed by a long career working on endowment advisory projects in the US and internationally. She's a Stanford University Distinguished Careers Institute Fellow, and lives in Exeter, NH and Boston, MA.

CPSIA information can be obtained
at www.ICGtesting.com
Printed in the USA
LVHW101023050422
715348LV00004B/136

9 781643 886114